Herd of Nightmares

Kerry E. B. Black

Printed in the United States of America

First Printing 2018

ISBN 13: 978-1-948894-02-9
ISBN10: 1-948894-02-5

Tree Shadow Press

www.treeshadowpress.com

For reproduction permission, contact:
Kerry E. B. Black
https://kerrylizblack.wordpress.com

Cover art by Chris Blickenderfer.
Author photo by C.A. Black

DEDICATION

For Deb and Laura, the good folk at
Carrot Ranch, Andy and Dyl, Susana,
Sarah, Ruth, Matthew, and Alexi,
And of course, for Mom,
because it all begins with Mom.

But most of all, for you,
dear readers and riders,
with heart-felt thanks.

CONTENTS

ACKNOWLEDGMENTS

At one time or another, most writers I know doubt their ability to write. I'm no exception. Several of these collected stories were previously published and I'm so grateful to their publishers. That they saw fit to print my words within their publications lent validity to my many hours of effort.

Along those lines, my editor at Tree Shadow Press, Deb Sanchez, encouraged and believed in me even when I might have given up on my dreams.

I've found support from my Birches, The Circle, Writers World, and Writers' Refuge among other online groups, and most emphatically I'm grateful to my friends within the Nomadic Wordsters.

And of course, without the support, encouragement, and understanding of my family, I'd never have written anything at all.

Nightmares

They stamp and paw with impatience grey and spongy ground, mining with shredded hooves the deepest frights and latent fears. These great, skeletal beasts labor under the loose command of Morpheus. Night-hags sometimes mount bareback and naked, gripping matted manes prone to drift into the collective subconscious. Demons lust for them, but over millennia, herbivorous teeth sharpened to tiger-like grips, herds run wild without a stallion.

Hetty's Hate

Hetty wanted to punch him in the gut and watch him double over. Then when he looked up at her, confused and angry, punch him in the nose and feel his blood squelch over her fist. Instead, she hid her hands within the sleeves of her too-big shirt and controlled her breathing, to all appearances the dutiful daughter.

"See, it's for the best. We don't need her, anyway," her father said.

She wished her glare could burn a hole through his dishonest heart. Yes, they did need her. Hetty needed her. Without her, all of the household responsibilities fell on Hetty's thirteen-year-old shoulders. She turned away from him and gathered the dishes from dinner.

Hetty scraped the uneaten spaghetti into the trash and sunk the soiled dishes and cutlery in the soapy water in the sink. Her hands warmed as she sought the washrag beneath the bubbles and set to scrubbing.

Her father ran his hand through his thinning, grey hair, pushing it from his flushed face. He resembled an anorexic Einstein after, hair standing on end. She tried to ignore him, but his every movement annoyed her.

How many women's hearts did he think he could win? She swiped each tine of the sterling, removing any trace of her dad's latest conquest. She ran her finger along the rim of the crystal, assured that the woman's lipstick left no waxy residue.

He sighed. "I think I'll go to the bar."

She longed to admonish him. *Don't you think you've had enough tonight?*

His eyes resembled a pink-eye patient's, and his nose glowed red. He stunk of stale wine, and droplets of the latest red stained his front.

The clock showed a cheery weekend six o'clock. He could find another tonight if he cleaned up a bit and put on the musky cologne to mask the smells of stale drink and broken heart. Father required diversion and attention. Another could help around the house and, if clever, might claim his affections for longer than a month.

"I'll call a cab," she said with a quiet voice. "You should change your shirt and mind your manicure."

He considered his hands. "Yeah, you're right." He sounded distracted.

She threw the drying towel over the cleaned pots. *I hate that I have to do the clean-up.* She dialed the taxi company with the standard instructions, then set to work, donning an apron left by one of her father's conquests.

Better I do it, I guess. He'd make a mess of things, anyways.

The cabbie beeped his arrival. She wiped her hands on the apron and watched him fuss before the hallway mirror before departing. His hair lay tidy and his clothes befitted a wealthy playboy. She stood on tiptoes to apply a bit of concealer to disguise the redness of his nose. Visine, cologne, and Garden Gate

Mechanic's Soap worked their magic.

"Thanks, Pudding," he said. He touched his index finger to her nose. His hands smelled of rosemary and lye. "You have this under control?"

Her neck hurt as she craned to look into his blue eyes. Many of the women thought them bright and welcoming, like a summer sky. Hetty knew the truth. Their blue served as a premonition of their demises. "Don't I always take care of everything, Daddy?"

His smile displayed perfect teeth. "Yes, you do."

She shuffled her feet, leaving arching patterns in the nape of the carpet. She feared meeting his gaze. "If you bring another one home, one who helps with the housework, can we keep her a bit longer, do you think, please?"

"For a while." His words thrilled her. He cupped her chin and kissed her forehead. "You do a lot to help your old dad. You're my only true girl."

Her stomach lurched. She took a shallow breath, fearful that a deep one might loosen the bindings she wrapped about her ribcage. Hetty wondered if by growing, she might lose his "true girl" designation. As much as she hated him, she couldn't bear that.

By an instinct, she flattened the burgeoning curves springing from her chest, squelched signs of adolescence without mercy. In the others, the conquests, something about buxom tops and tiny waists inspired his desire. When he tired of their perky bouncing, he worked around pretty lingerie to extract what he wanted and leave it on a platter to be preserved.

When the taxi's tail lights retreated like a hellhound hiding among tombs, she finished the cleaning. He preferred his women small, which made tidying up a bit easier. She grabbed a mason jar and twisted its cold, two-part lid. She wrinkled her nose when the formaldehyde stunk up the dining area. It made a plop as she poured the heart from the serving dish into the jar and secured the lid. She marked it with the date, then put it with the others in the pantry.

A Thought

Ever wonder what happened to all the mothers in fairy tales? So few survived to see their daughters grow to beauties. They never imparted wisdom, never gave their warnings. Happily ever after is fleeting. Once found, it claims its participants and hands them to its cohort.

Death.

Red Spots

Liza woke with a scream. Although the dream's details fled with the daylight, an unshakable feeling of foreboding dogged her thoughts. Worrisome spots floated before her vision. Her hands shook as she prepared a pot of strong coffee instead of her typical spiced green tea. The bitter liquid warmed but did not wash away her unease.

She turned the sign on the door to open and flipped a switch to light up her neon Hamsa sign. Some of the green gas needed replacement, leaving the eye only partially illuminated. *Need to call about that.*

She lit sandalwood candles, and myrrh incense floated Heavenward like prayers. The bell tinkled, announcing her first client. She glanced at the small bundle of sage and lavender. *Wish I could've smudged first. Oh well.*

The scent of citrus greeted her, and a weak smile crossed Liz's face. "Mrs. Greenstein! How lovely to see you again!"

The slumped old lady took her customary cushioned seat at the round table in the corner. Liz pulled a shawl from a peg and wrapped it around her shoulders and took the seat opposite. Mrs. Greenstein's wrinkled, squashed face resembled an over-ripe apple, sunken and discolored, but her smile shone genuine and her money sat in the cut crystal donation bowl.

Liz fought to clear her disjointed thoughts. "What can I do for you today, dear?"

The old lady's voice quavered, high pitched and fragile. "It's my grandchildren."

"Ah," said Liz.

She extended her hands across the table, sending her bangle bracelets clanging like alarm bells. As Mrs. Greenstein's papery skin touched her palms, images swam before Liz's closed eyes.

"Your stomach's been bothering you again, hasn't it, dear?"

"Yes, but it's nothing."

I wish it was. Liz saw the cancer spreading through the old lady's body like a storm.

"The girl whose name starts with a 'P' is expecting a baby."

"Oh, that's Penny! But wait, she's not married yet."

Liz opened her eyes and saw Mrs. Greenstein's worried expression.

"Oh, perhaps she's only wishing for a baby."

The old lady pushed her thin lips together before saying, "When?"

"When?"

"When's the child to arrive?"

Liz scrutinized the resolve in her client's weathered face. "Spring. April."

Mrs. Greenstein nodded, lips set in a tight line.

Liz's lids slid closed, and she interpreted the flashes she perceived. "Spots."

"Spots?"

"I am sorry. I keep seeing spots. Red, in irregular patterns on a pale background. Red spots."

The old woman gasped. "The measles! I keep telling my fool granddaughter to get her kids vaccinated, but she won't. Wait 'til I see her!" Mrs. Greenstein shook with indignation and fatigue.

"I think that's all for today."

"That's quite enough. Thank you, Lizabelle."

Liz placed a gentle kiss on Mrs. Greenstein's soft cheek. *This will be the last time I see her*. On impulse, she wrapped the little lady in an embrace and whispered, "Thank you for being one of my best patrons."

Mrs. Greenstein stiffened with surprise, stepped back, and nodded. "Take care."

She watched Mrs. Greenstein limp out of the door, her grey raincoat blending in with the morning fog, until she disappeared from view.

She dusted her beloved trinkets and fluffed the pillows. Everywhere, from within the rich, warm Middle Eastern patterns of the rug to the intricate designs of the silk hangings, she imagined those crimson spots.

Her next client entered in a hurry, anxious lest someone see her visiting such a shop. She smelled of cinnamon, cigarettes, and hairspray. Her twitchy movements belied her need for a caffeine fix.

"Tea?" Liz offered as she poured a cup.

A blush rose in the woman's rouged cheeks, and she licked the lipstick from her lips. Her hand trembled as she accepted the china cup and saucer.

"Thank you."

"You're welcome."

The woman took a sip, returned the cup to the saucer, and said, "I've been told you speak to the dead."

"Yes."

"How much does it cost?"

"The suggested donation chart hangs there." Liz pointed an amethyst-ringed finger at the wall.

The lady squinted, set the tea things on a nearby table, and took the amount from her wallet.

Liz's hand floated like a bindi-dancer's. "Please take a seat."

The women joined hands, and Liz closed her eyes.

"Spots. Again, red spots on a white background."

The woman gasped. "Yes, my mother. She was buried in a red polka-dotted dress."

Liz concentrated. "Her name starts with an 'S.'"

Tears rolled over the woman's cheeks. "Yes. Stella."

"Stella of the stars. She's here with you. She asks if you remembered to feed the dog."

The woman laughed until she coughed.

"She wants you to stop smoking."

Sobered, the woman narrowed her eyes, "My mother smoked her whole life."

"Yes, she admits that, but she wants you to live. Forty-two is too young to die."

A gurgling sound escaped the woman. "She was forty-two when she died."

"She doesn't want family history repeated."

The woman chewed until the red lipstick speckled her teeth. Her plucked brows turned nose-ward, and she asked, "Can she tell me where Daddy's accounts are? We can't find them, and his Alzheimer's is worse."

A number swam between the red. Liz repeated it, feeling weightless. With a sigh, she rubbed her temples.

"I'm sorry. You've got to go now."

"What do that number mean?"

"I don't know." Her head pounded like bright ruby splashes. "Think on it. The meaning will come to you. Perhaps talk it over with your sisters and your brother."

The woman pushed back her chair. "I didn't tell you I have sisters, and we don't talk to my brother. Ever. He's a scum."

"I'm sorry. Good luck."

The woman left. Before the tinkling of the front door bells stopped, she'd reached into her pocket and retrieved her pack of cigarettes.

Liz slumped into the chair and dozed.

The bell announced another shop visitor. Liz opened her eyes to see a plain-faced, dark-haired man. She forced a smile and pulled herself to her feet.

"Hello, may I help you?"

The man stared, chewing his lip, without saying a word.

"My services and suggested donations are outlined there." She pointed to the calligraphed plaque.

He nodded and stepped further into the room.

The red spots swam in her vision. Liz rubbed a hand over her eyes, hoping to clear the effect.

"My sister comes here to see you."

Liz scrutinized his face. There was something familiar in the plains of his cheeks.

"What can I do for you today?"

He touched a set of crystal wind chimes, setting them in musical motion.

"Tell me what you told her."

"Who, your sister? What's her name?"

"Don't play with me. What did you tell her?"

"I see many people." The woman who just left, the woman with the numbers and the cigarettes. "Do you mean the lady who just left?"

"Of course I do. Some psychic you are."

The red spots on the white background reached toward her.

"Your mother wore red polka dots to her funeral."

"I don't care. I didn't go to her funeral."

Her ears rang. "I gave her some numbers, but I don't know what they mean." She repeated them.

His voice sounded dangerous as a snake's hiss. "I do.

She did not feel the blade. Shock insulated her, but an unmistakable fountain of garnet erupted from her neck. The geyser speckled every surface, high and low. She tried to talk, but only gurgling sounds escaped the gaping hole in her throat. She fell to the ground. The white ceiling dominated her vision, white speckled with red, white tin decorated with droplets of her blood falling from their perch to speckle her prone body. The door bells announced he left the shop. Her only company as she died were splashes of her own blood.

Haiku 1

Some nightmares sprout wings

When washed in dawn's staining rays -

Others rend, unbound

Bronzed

Barry always hated the bronze fairy statue, with its Nuevo-slimness and pert expression. His wife, Jennifer, adored the thing. She insisted it grace a spot on the mantle in the living room where its dark patina greeted guests like a black hole.

"It's an antique, Barry. Been in the family forever."

He cast baleful glances at its feminine wistfulness. Hard to enjoy a night of sports with the guys while Princess Prissy Pantless (which he despairingly dubbed the thing) blew her ocarina. Just embarrassing!

"Can we put it someplace else?"

She squelched his hope-filled suggestion. "No. It needs to be there where I can always see it."

He groaned. "It gives me the creeps, Jen."

She stood on tip-toes to kiss him. "You know my Grandma gave it to me, right? She said it protects us women. It belonged to her Great-Grandma."

He kissed her forehead. "All right, all right."

Jenny's ex-husband had filed a series of lawsuits, harrying Barry's wife with custody and monetary modifications. By lying to the children and calling their mother a witch whose family ate men, her ex made Jenny's life uncomfortable. The kids returned from visits with him angry, frightened, and distressed.

Jenny often dissolved into tears. "I can't deal with this! It's not fair! I don't malign him. Why's he doing it to me?"

"I don't know, but try not to worry. Things will work out. You'll see."

Barry felt like someone watched his movements. When he sought the source, nothing but the fairy statue greeted his gaze.

After a particularly bad day, Jenny desired solitary time instead of snuggling in bed after the evening news.

"You go on. I just want to sit here and think."

He woke alone in the wee hours and followed the echoes of her muttering something about "just say the word." He found her curled on the couch, hugging her knees, staring toward the fireplace. Embers revealed her tear-stained face.

Barry sat, wrapping her slim form in an embrace.

"Honey, you can't do this to yourself."

"I know. It's just I feel so un-empowered. He's turning my kids against me."

"Not really. They're too smart for that."

"Did you hear what they said to me tonight? They called me weak. Said I don't take good enough care of them. Donny accused my family of murdering their husbands. Imagine! When I asked why he thought such a sickening thing, he said his dad told him."

"Sweetheart, don't let it get to you. The kids will come around, and all this worry's no good." He kissed the top of her head, inhaling the coconut scent of her shampoo.

"You don't understand," she whispered.

He cupped her chin and gazed into her eyes. "I don't. Not really. But I know I love you. And this is wrecking your well-being.

If you're not healthy, you can't be strong. The kids need their strong momma."

She nestled into his chest.

"I love you," she said.

A flame kindled on the grate, making the bronze fairy's shadow dance around the room like an angry moth.

Jenny sighed. "You're right, of course. This is not healthy." She swallowed, sat up, and nodded toward the hearth. "It's time."

They closed the fire behind safety glass doors and retired.

Barry dreamed a bird flew down the chimney and crashed into the walls, seeking escape. When his dream-self opened the door, the bird stabbed him with its viscous beak.

He woke with a start. Jenny's hair fanned across the pillow, framing her peaceful visage. Steady breathing told his jump did not rouse her. He smiled. *Such a beautiful wife.*

A loud knock at the front door demanded attention.

Jenny woke with a start.

Barry rolled out of bed and slid on his slippers. "Stay here. I'll get it."

Two uniformed police officers filled the front porch. "We need to see your wife."

Barry showed them in. "I'll get Jenny."

She dressed with haste and joined them.

The four perched on the living room furniture.

"Please tell us what is going on," Barry said.

The uniformed men exchanged glances. "Can you account for your whereabouts last night, Ma'am?"

She startled and looked at him. "Here. On the couch or in the bed all night. Why?"

"Can anyone verify that?"

"Me," Barry said, furrowing his brow.

"You were here all night as well, Sir?"

"Yes. What's this all about?"

"Ma'am, your ex-husband was murdered last night in his apartment. Blunt force trauma, repeated blows with something small, like a ball-peen hammer."

Her hand flew to her opened mouth. "Oh," she exclaimed. She looked ceiling-ward, above the mantle.

"Did he have any enemies?"

Jenny grabbed Barry's hand. It trembled.

"I-I don't know. We've been divorced for nine years come September. I only talk to him about the kids."

"You have two children, right? I boy and a girl? Ten and twelve?"

Jenny widened her eyes and her voice broke. "Oh, God, how am I going to tell them their Dad is dead?"

She buried her face in Barry's shoulder and wept. Barry found comfort in the fact that the kids always slept late when given the opportunity.

The men shifted on their seats, staring around the room, careful to avoid the crying woman. Barry patted his wife's quaking shoulder. Something seemed displaced on the mantle.

The older officer cleared his throat. "We're sorry, Ma'am. We just a few more questions, then we'll be on our way." He flipped through his notebook. "Your ex-husband filed a series of lawsuits recently, right?"

Jenny sniffed, wiping her nose. She nodded. "Yeah." She gasped and the color drained from her face.

Barry's mouth gaped. "Surely you don't think Jenny had anything to do with...that?"

The younger officer cleared his throat. He looked at his polished shoes. "Of course not, sir. We have to ask."

They stood, closing their notebooks. "Sorry to convey such bad news, Ma'am. Please call if anything occurs to you."

Jenny sniffed back tears, her nose and eyes red. Barry squeezed her shoulder then showed the officers out.

He rested his head against the door after they left. It felt cool and solid against his forehead. He forced his mind to work through the sluggishness of confused information.

Jenny hiccupped.

She needs me.

He slid beside her, encircling her waist with his arm. "You okay?"

"Uh-huh." Her voice sounded distant.

"What are we going to tell the kids?"

"Dunno." She continued to stare. "Barry, we were together all night long."

He drew his eyebrows together. "Yeah."

"Did you get rid of my fairy?"

"What?"

She pointed. The ever-present fairy statue was missing.

Young Blood

Trees' roots run deep, sopping up the blood of ancestors. They do not discriminate, these networked fingers, in their quest for nourishment. Their preferred sustenance, though, is that which pumped through human forms, and in the oldest of woods, the taste is refined. While no meal will be left unsampled, the oldest ones crave young blood.

The newspapers fed the public's fascination with the case. Jacob Miller of Enchiton, Pennsylvania claimed that he sold his four-year-old sister to an ugly elf. He stood, pale and slight, a scrawny, dark-haired boy of ten whose head did not clear the second panel of the judge's mahogany bench.

Judge Kathleen Santiago had the dubious distinction of sitting the case.

"I have listened to myriad psychiatric testimony regarding this case. The evidence points to a child involved in murder, though we have no body. A family stands to lose not one but two children."

She glanced at the parents sitting in the front row behind their son, just as pale. Neither looked as though they slept recently, with their red-rimmed and over-bright eyes circled by purple and grey puffy rings.

"It is my decision," the grave Justice intoned, "that Jacob Miller be held for further evaluation at the county psychiatric hospital."

Cameras flashed.

Mrs. Miller, Jacob's mother, hissed, "No!"

Her husband caught his pregnant wife as she collapsed.

The judge pounded her gavel, saying, "Order in the court."

The public in the gallery, however, disobeyed.

Yells of "Murderer!" battled with "He's just a little boy."

The bailiff escorted Jacob, whose head hung limp, from the courtroom.

"Go home, Sasha!" Jacob said, scrambling down a hill in the woods behind his house.

"No, Jacob, Momma said I stay with you." Sasha's blonde curls bobbed as she struggled to keep up with her big brother. Her plump legs worked, and she exchanged her typical sunny face for a scowl.

"You're such a pest! Leave me alone!" Down-ward facing brows darkened his narrowed eyes.

He negotiated through brush to a clearing ringed with tall deciduous trees. He pulled his satchel over his head and dropped it with a clang and thud on the mossy ground. A brook gurgled over algae-covered rocks in the east. Birds' songs and insect chirps formed musical duets. Violets colored the sparse grass, while wild flowers of white, purple, and pink perfumed the moist, late-spring air.

Sasha plopped on the ground beneath an elm, crushing two toadstools as she sat, cross-legged. Her lower lip jutted in a profound pout, elbows pressed her knees, while her chin rested on her palms, disgruntled.

Jacob ignored her and set to work. Near the brook, close to the trunk of a large weeping willow, rested a pile of scavenged building supplies, cast-offs dumped in the woods by neighbors after remodeling projects. He hauled wood of various sizes and laid it out in the center of the clearing, matching pieces. He separated rotten pieces he hoped would hold together for his project.

From the bag, he extracted a plastic container of nails and his father's hammer. Then he started constructing his cabin. When finished, it would stand about the size of a dog's house, he imagined, just big enough to escape the world for a while. He could read comics by flashlight or sort his baseball cards. He'd drag a plastic bin from his bedroom to hold things like toy cars. He sighed, contended, thinking about the private retreat.

Privacy grew more precious with each passing day. His parents demanded he "shoulder more responsibilities" since he was the oldest. His mom expected another baby in a few months. They said that when the baby came, if it was a boy, he'd need to share his room. If it was a girl, Sasha would have a new roommate.

Sasha already popped in to his room nightly, asking if he would play with her. Sasha did not respect his privacy. If that baby was a boy, he would never be alone. He needed quiet time to think.

Jacob smacked his fingers with a misplaced hammer blow. He winced and shook his hand. Sasha laughed. "Did you bang it, Jacob?" she giggled.

"No, I felt like shaking my hand, you dummy."

"Hey, don't call me names, Jacob. It's not nice."

"Well, it's not nice to laugh at me, either." He thrust his fingers into his mouth.

He regarded his little sister. She looked like mom, sunny like a California beach. Everyone commented on her beauty. Her cuteness.

They did not have to put up with her.

They did not compliment him, either.

Using his best persuasive voice, he asked, "Sasha, why don't you just go home?" He opened his eyes wide, trying to look innocent. "Don't you have some dolls that you want to play with or something?" He smiled to encourage her. *Please, Sasha, take the bait*, he thought.

"Nope. I'm staying."

She resumed her inspection of a bit of foliage and hummed "Itsy Bitsy Spider," ignoring her brother's glare.

A wind rose and blew the shaky walls over. Jacob stomped and threw his father's hammer to the ground. It bounced on the moss, ricocheted off of a rock, and hit Sasha on the knee.

She wailed, "You did that on purpose, Jacob! I'm telling Mom!"

He hopped over to her, bouncing from leg to leg, hand to his lips. "No, I didn't mean it to hit you, Sasha! Wait! Don't tattle, please!"

She ran, though, chubby legs pumping up the hill and out of sight. He scrambled to catch up but slipped on a yellow and orange mushroom, smearing it into the loam. Mud marked his blue jeans and palms.

"Great," he thought, "Do I go after her or just wait for my punishment?"

From behind him, Jacob heard a rustling like wind blowing old leaves. He looked over his shoulder, then started. A little man stepped from the shadow of an oak near the brook. He stood about Jacob's height, but the wrinkles on his visage belied advanced age. His grey hair fell in scraggly knots to his stooped shoulders, and he wore a loose-fitting linen shirt tucked into dirty pants, belted with twine.

The little man scuffled to the cabin, tut-tutting over the fallen walls. Jacob faced him, Sasha and his pending punishment forgotten. "Hey mister, what are you doing here?"

The man looked over his long, pointed nose. His eyes sparkled a startling green.

"What is your name, boy?" he asked.

Jacob considered. He knew better than to talk to a stranger, but something about this man intrigued him. "Jacob," he answered, "Jacob Miller." The man nodded.

"You building a house for yerself?" he asked the boy, pointing a twig-like thumb at the attempt.

Jacob nodded, pressing his lips in a disappointed moue.

"I can help you with it, if ye want," said the old man. He cocked his head at an odd angle. "Just cost you yer sister."

Jacob's head snapped up. His back stiffened.

He said, "What? What are you talking about, mister?"

The senior leaned in, shifted wood and supplies.

"See, I can build a nice house fer you. Would you want a doorway pointing to the east, to greet the sun when she's a'risin'? And a couple of windows with glass panes to keep the breeze out? A sloped roof like this," He motioned with gnarled hands, "and a small staircase to give you some storage up in a balcony."

Jacob pictured the place there in the glen, a hide-away where he could spend time unsupervised and uninterrupted. With snacks, a sleeping bag, a flashlight and lighter, he could live here on his own. He could drink from the brook, too.

"That sounds real nice, mister," Jacob said, brushing some of the drying mud from his palms, "but what do you mean about Sasha?"

The old fellow's face split in a crooked smile. His teeth were decaying and sharp-edged. He stepped closer to Jacob, leaned close to his face. Jacob smelt decay wafting from the odd man's mouth.

"I love little girls, Jacob."

The brother crossed whitish arms over his thin chest, his jaw and lips pressed. "Everyone loves Sasha," he thought.

Head tilted to his side, the elderly fellow considered Jacob. "I can help you. I like young boys, too. And I think I really like you."

He smiled again, a wicked, lopsided smirk. He extended his weathered hand in the universal motion of acceptance.

Jacob considered, then extended his own immature hand. The old guy's palm felt rough and dry, like ancient tree bark. Although dirty, Jacob's looked stark and white by contrast, like a grub pulled from the ground. They shook a deal, and then Jacob turned to make his way home.

Mother stood in the doorway, glowering, hands on her rounded belly, looming over her son with a frown.

"You are in big trouble, little man. What were you thinking? Sasha's too little to walk through the woods on her own!"

Sasha peeked from behind her mother's legs. She stuck her plump, pink tongue out at her brother.

Jacob narrowed his eyes at her. *Pest*, he thought, but aloud he said, "Mom, I'm sorry. She ran away."

Besides, I am too young to babysit that little brat, he thought. "I asked her to stop, but she would not listen to me," He said.

Sasha tugged on the hem of her mother's skirt. "Momma, he throwed a bambber at me."

"I did not!" he directed to Sasha, then turned his attention to his glowering mother, whining, "I was frustrated and threw the hammer, yes, but not at her. It bounced and barely bumped her!"

Mother sighed. She reached a trembling hand to her temple and rubbed, closing her blood-shot eyes.

"Look at her! There isn't ever a mark on her. If I threw a hammer at her, there would be a mark."

His mother looked at her boy, placid, then turned and with long strides, reached the powder room to throw up. Great heaving, sloppy sounds. Sasha stood in the hallway outside, worry written on her small face.

Mother emerged, shaking, wiping her lips with a pink hand towel.

Jacob sidled to her. "I am sorry, Mom."

Mother opened her eyes and managed a watery smile. "I'm just so tired, Jacob. It would be a tremendous help if you and Sasha would get along and play together for a little while so that I can rest."

"Okay, Mom, I got it." His eyelids slid to obscure his baby blues. He swallowed, hard, then said, "Sasha, come with me. I have something that I am working on in the woods."

Haiku 2

Slipping in and out

Happy little devil child

Dancing dimensions

Maleficium

We hailed from a land where our features were as doughy as the beads that sustained us. Our backs were broad, because we carried many burdens, yet we were noble-born, educated, and inclined to learn quickly, for our very existence depended upon our alacrity.

This English land of cold and rain, preferable to our own austere Germanic homes, was fraught with perils. When my mistress, Anne, arrived from Cleves to marry the notorious King Henry VIII, a masquerade greeted her. Language barriers and difference in upbringing made the match difficult. The King expressed displeasure, but he kissed sweet Anne upon her cheek as she rose and before she retired for the night.

Still, the King favored a pretty, young English girl for his bride, an assigned maid of honor from a good family, and King Henry VIII always got his way.

Anne's divorce settlements suited her, suited us all, but we were well aware that the masked ball continued despite the presumably discarded disguises. Music and gaiety, the pulse of the court, left all subjected to the King's changeable whims.

We learned to refine our English and adapt our skills to those of the Tudor court. Poetry, courtly admiration, and dance replaced domestic arts when thrust in that glittering, raucous realm. For her compliance, Anne was honored as "King's sister" and given lands, including Hever Castle and its grounds, Seale, and Kemsing. A respectable household traveled with and served my Lady. We were, many of us, from Schloss Burg and Cleves.

Ours was a household-at-the ready. When the royal whim struck, we needed to glitter like crown jewels. Otherwise, we managed the properties and household with day-to-day diligence, often with less money and materials than necessary.

The royal daughters visited often, and their stays brought welcome brightness.

A letter from the pretty, intelligent, red-haired Elizabeth announced a short stay on her way to visit her father's court. We exalted in preparation for her stopover. It provided a celebration, and with gusto, we set to work.

"We need fresh rushes for the dining hall, please, and vases of flowers to scent the rooms! Forget-me-nots are in bloom. And roses for the Princess' chambers."

Pomanders need to be filled, ladies. Good scents, please. I like sandalwood."

The grooms must prepare the stalls for the guests' mounts with fresh straw and alfalfa hay."

"But where are Mr. and Mrs. Broickhuser?"

Mistress Anne's whippet hound capered underfoot, fascinated by the activities and new smells. She hunched her bony back and skittered under the buffet table, her long nails clicking.

"Someone please get the sapphire collar for the dog."

Heavenly smells of cooking wafted through the front halls closest to the kitchen. The spices in rich sauces smelled exotic, so different from the typical, rustic meals we normally consumed. My stomach rumbled, anticipating the meal.

"Sweets prepared, meats seasoned, peacocks baked and ready to be re-feathered. The feast will be spectacular!" The cook declared, chest puffed with pride, face ruddy with exertion.

We cleaned and starched our white linen collars and cuffs, brushed the velvets to bring up the pile, and polished our few treasured jewels. The household buzzed with excitement. Girls giggled. Men fidgeted. Women attended to final details to impress the some-time princess. (Her status depended on her father's mood.)

Yet despite being caught up in the activities of the castle, my head ached. Something nagged at the recesses of my mind like a scarcely-heard scratching of rodents in the larder. I smiled through my discomfort.

By the time dusk painted charcoals across the sky, however, we realized the daughter of Henry's shamed second wife would not be joining us. Frowns and downcast eyes transformed decorated faces, and shoulders slumped with defeat. Sighs mingled with the growing gloom.

Mistress Anne smiled at us, disguising her own disappointment. We were no strangers to disappointment, but we also called resilience our companion. Head high, shoulders squared, Anne's brown eyes sparkled. She clapped her hands together, her ring capturing the torchlight. In silent obedience, we regarded her.

"Well, we have worked hard to prepare a party, so let us enjoy a party! My dears, tuck in!"

To entertain Princess Elizabeth, we had sent for minstrels. Though we lacked the guest of honor, local performers dressed in motley sung ballads for their suppers.

"My mistress' eyes shine bright into my own, and roses in her cheeks reside..."

A juggler and a contortionist displayed their skills.

I clapped along with my fellows, but beneath the fresh scents of flowers and feast, a waft of sulfur and charred carbon assaulted my nose, and a feeling of foreboding sat heavy upon my shoulders. I shifted to the left on my wooden seat, seeking some comfort, but there was no bending in my corset.

Ever astute, my mistress Anne set a gentle hand upon the fur of my folded-back sleeve. "You seem uncomfortable. If you wish to retire, you have permission." A maternal smile reassured me, and I bowed my head in gratitude.

Curtseying, I took my leave. Their voices haunted the stone hallways as I retreated to the gardens, hoping to revive with the night air. The knot garden spilled rosemary, thyme, and lavender, and roses line the walkway. White pebbles crunched beneath each step. Bats careened after insects overhead, dipping and soaring in an awkward, deadly dance.

My beaded, black velvet French hood felt heavy, pressing in on my temples, and my dainty shoes bit into the sides of my feet, so I sat on a sheltered marble bench near a garden pond in which lilies bloomed. I closed my eyes and willed the tension to leave my body.

The smell of rotting eggs drifted with the fog, enveloping me. On impulse, I slid further into the shadow of the bench, my dark dress and cloak hiding me from view. My pulse pumped as though I'd run, and I fought to quiet my breathing.

Someone - or something - haunted the garden path.

It was difficult to identify the cause of my unease. Certainly, another of the household could be enjoying the pathways. Something about the change of the air, though, set my hair on end beneath my clothing. My eyes strained as I sought to identify the figures approaching.

Two people, a man and a woman, in proper, courtly attire strolled, but something in their movements betrayed them. The woman walked too free of confinement, and the man stalked like one of the panthers kept in London's tower. Their heads jerked at odd angles, and their hushed tones carried alarming messages.

"Princess pudding is mighty nice!"

"I like royal flesh the best, but I am angry enough to eat the inferiors in there. How dare that flame-haired brat not show? Without a note of explanation, too."

"I can braid her hair into falls. Red is much in favor these days. Red falls to sell in market when the meat is gone."

With quiet care, I pulled my feet under the bench. The sulfuric stench choked me, but I held my breath to keep from coughing. They stood within ten feet of my hiding place, conversing as they stripped a thin branch of its leaves.

"What use was possessing these two if we haven't access to that Elizabeth? I am so angry I could burn this refuse to the ground." The woman motioned with her left hand toward Hever Castle where my mistress and her household frolicked. She threw the leaves, their silvery undersides flashing like fish in the moonlight.

The man twisted his head at an unnatural slant, and the moonlight revealed a familiar face.

I stifled a gasp.

Mr. Jasper Broickhuser, a member of the household, looked ill. His eyes sunk into a pale face. His cheekbones jutted, stretching sallow skin that pooled along his jawline. His lips pulled back from his over-large teeth in a sneer, and his hands twisted into claws.

I dared not move and scarcely breathed, fearing my heart would burst within my breast. If that was Jasper, then the woman must be his wife, Gertrude. I scrutinized her form. It was, indeed.

"Let us leave. There are sisters dabbling in the craft at the King's castle. We can take over their bodies and get close to a princess."

"Being surrounded by the royal court will make accessing our chosen feast difficult. Too many people about. That's why this situation was ideal."

"Ah, but the people at court are self-absorbed, and the princesses are often out of favor. In fact, the pig-faced king is mooning after his "Rose without Thorns," and she doesn't care for Mary or Elizabeth."

"True. As long as the King's head is turned, few tend to the discarded bastard children. The princesses must feel so neglected!" Their cold laughs echoed around the fountain.

"It should not be difficult to lure a lonely girl."

"Flatter, entice. We can, indeed."

"Then, when we have her alone, we will have our way. Fresh princess meat!"

The two put their heads together and gave a chilling laugh akin to dog yips. They reached skyward, and the foul-smelling fog spiraled around and shrouded their forms. As the fog rose up, an unsettling glee reverberated overhead.

Jasper and Gertrude's bodies fell insensible to the pathway with a loud thud.

A shudder wracked my body. I left the husband and wife where they lay and ran, muscles freed from the rigor mortis of fear. Panting, since my whalebone stays made deep breaths impossible, I ignored waves of tremors. My consciousness swam and faded, but I shook with purpose when I at last reached my destination.

"Please help," I gasped.

Mistress Anne and two maids of honor rushed to my side.

I related what I witnessed. My words sobered the assembled in an instant. The butler and two footmen rushed to the garden. We exited the festive hall to investigate the Broickhuser's rooms.

Our approach sounded through the hallways, precursors to judgement. We knew the dangers associated with dark sorcery, witchcraft, and demon summoning. To avoid suspicion and investigation of the entire household required discretion. The involvement of the Inquisitors must be avoided. Though innocent, in their eyes, we would forever be suspected.

The Broickhusers kept their receiving room tidy and unremarkable. A small desk, a swept fireplace, a frame for needlework in progress. Nothing to indicate nefarious deeds.

The bedchamber with its heavy tapestry hangings and dark, carved wood, likewise appeared free of evils.

My headache worsened with a deeper conviction. "Something's here, and we must find it." I rubbed my temples.

We fanned out to conduct our search. It did not take long before we found an incriminating object. Under the bed rested a black leather tome with a sinister aspect. We dared not touch it, but instead used the iron poker from the hearth to push it into the room.

A sulfuric odor persisted, grew stronger in the wardrobe storage. We gasped. One of the ladies fainted, and the other pulled her aside to tend to her. I crossed myself

A star within a circle with wicked-looking symbols along the outside was etched into the stained oak floor between gowns and robes and belts and shifts. Tallow candles left char marks and grease at each star point.

We all stared and shivered. The Mistress of the castle then ordered the symbols filed from the floor.

She cleared her throat and turned to me. "Tell me again what the fiends said."

I repeated my recollections.

We confined the Broickhusers. My mistress sent for the vicar before she collected parchment, quills, and ink.

"We must mind the wording, that none question my motives or sanity, yet protect the Princesses. I will outline the happenings and request the dismissal and trial of the Broickhusers, of course."

King Henry VIII ignored her correspondence, but both Mary and Elizabeth sent genuine thank you letters with small gifts. The King's lack of attention presented a problem, because our household could not be altered without His Most Exalted's express permission. Although we kept them confined, none of us felt comfortable with the Broickhusers in residence.

Anne wrote to her brother in Cleves, pleading for assistance. When he at last wrote to Henry the King of England of the Broickhusers "driving mad with marvelous impostures and incantations" our entire household, the hateful conjurers were at last relieved of their duties.

I do not believe they were tried for sorcery, though, nor do I know if the sisters at the Royal Court who likewise dabbled in demon summoning were discovered.

I know only that no fiends ate the delightful Elizabeth and her serious sister Mary.

Haiku 3

Princess or pauper

Death doesn't discriminate

All end up the same

Malfeasance

Winnie hastened through the campus walkway, entering the slick, titanium-and-glass lecture hall, careful to hold her treasure against her body. The book's presence set her heart to racing. "Stupid place to meet if you have a secret," she thought, glaring at the transparent room divisions.

Joan stood and approached. "Winnie, nice to see you. What was so urgent, though, that it couldn't wait until after dinner?"

Winnie took her elbow and guided Joan back to the campus grounds. Even with the impeccable landscaping, it felt wilder, more appropriate there. After scouting to be sure they were unobserved, she slid the book from under her jumper.

Joan leaned in and then recoiled. "Oh my gosh, is that what I think it is? A book? I thought they were all burned as fire hazards after implant tablets were standard issue. Where did you find one?"

"It was at the bottom of an ancient trunk in Great Uncle Broickhuser's attic. I snatched it right away along with some cool candles and things. You know, old-world stuff. Isn't it great?"

Joan held up a hand, shaking her head as though warding Winnie off. "Are you crazy? Not only is it illegal to have hand-held books, but look at it! I bet it is crawling with worms and dust mites. I can smell the mold. Get rid of that awful thing before you get into trouble."

"Don't you want to know what's inside?"

"Do you mean besides the bugs that those filthy things hold? No. Why don't you just upload the text into your implant tablet?" Joan tapped her right temple for emphasis.

Winnie dropped her gaze to the tome, its leather cover supple beneath her grip. The thick pages and hand-written script possessed grace and mastery no upload could convey. "It's art, and it's beautiful. Don't you ever wonder why we aren't allowed books?"

Joan gaped. "Books represent waste. Resources depleted because of man's selfish desire to master the world. Instead of imparting wisdom, those things show our ancestors' ignorance and disregard. Uploads are verified for accuracy. Books were notoriously full of errors. Uploads cost nearly nothing. The expense involved in creating books was astronomical in terms of money and the toll on the environment. Trees for wood and paper. Fires. They are highly flammable, you know. Carbon and binders for the ink. Animals died for the glue and leather."

Winnie hugged the volume to her chest. The heft of the book comforted Winnie. *Why couldn't she understand?* Gentle, looping script and woodcuts within the creamy pages portrayed arcane knowledge with craftsmanship and art.

Joan rattled the contents of her jumper pocket. "Besides, that thing stinks."

Winnie inhaled the musty, accumulated knowledge. "Stinks?"

"Yes, like sulfur. Get rid of it, or I'll report you myself."

Her anger flared. "I don't know why I thought you would get this, Joan. Obviously telling you about it was a mistake. Sorry to have trusted you."

Joan blinked, slow and controlled. She extended her hand. "Let me see it."

Winnie's grip tightened. "What? Why?"

"Just let me see it."

Maybe if she holds it, she'll understand. With reluctance, Winnie handed it to her friend.

"It has these sort of recipes inside. It is fascinating. I've never seen anything like it."

Joan's nose wrinkled as the volume dropped open in her arms, revealing a medieval illustration of an alchemical formula. "Oh, Winnie. This is nonsense." She threw the book to the path and cast an Armstrong's stick atop. Flames danced along the book.

"No!"

Joan tackled Winnie. She pinned her to the path, rendering her helpless. "It's for your own good, Winnie. You get these divergent ideas at times, and they aren't good for you or for society."

"Get off, please," Winnie sobbed, unable to push the larger girl from her. She closed her eyes, unwilling to witness the destruction. Once Winnie stopped struggling, Joan stood.

"It was for your own good, you know. You'd have landed in loads of trouble."

Winnie rubbed the red marks where Joan restrained her. She struggled to her feet, brushing pea-sized gravel from her jumper and hair. "I hate you."

Joan's face contorted with shock. Without a further word, she rushed up the path back to school.

Winnie glared at her retreating form. She turned to collect the ashes of her beloved book, but gasped. Despite its age and alleged flammability, the book remained intact. A golden glow illuminated the encircled star on the cover, as though the flame gilded it. Winnie knelt before it, cradled it beneath her clothing, and returned to her dormitory.

She locked the door against intrusion and sat cross-legged at the foot of her bed, the manuscript pulsing in her lap. With trembling hands, she opened it and read the wisdom of her ancestors. Time lost meaning. Ignoring hunger, schoolwork, and social obligations, Winnie soaked up un-sanitized, unauthorized information, her lust for deeper connection with the ancient, hidden world consuming her. During a restroom break, her deranged appearance surprised her. She ran fingers through the tangles in her neglected hair. Eyes stared red and watery through swollen, sleep-deprived lids. *How many days passed*?

She ignored insistent knocking from floormates as she pushed aside her moon chair to make space on the floor. With every bottle of red nail polish she owned, she imitated a design from the book. She lit her Great Uncle's candles and intoned the incantation, careful of interpretation. *My intentions are clear, even if I possess limited linguistics skills.* "Come to me. Use me as your vessel. Fill me with you, and together we can wipe out the malignancy of conformity."

A shadowy form coalesced from the darkness, its blackness growing solid. The faceless shape hissed, "Are there princesses? I long for princess pudding."

With a bemused smile, Winnie shook her head. "No princesses. Monarchies were done away with by the end of the last century. Even the pocket nations don't declare their dictators royal. Instead, our universal traits are acknowledged."

"So, you're all royal."

Winnie considered. "Perhaps. Or none of us are. In any case, nobody uses terms like princess any longer." She glanced through the haze rising from the candles to the book. "What am I supposed to do now?"

"Welcome me in."

"I did, didn't I, by performing this ritual?"

"Welcome me in to your heart and body. I will take possession of your soul."

"Soul? How provincial. What will you do with my body?"

"Share it with you. We'll fill voids and feed. Just step into the circle with me. Embrace me. I'll do the rest."

"Will it hurt?"

"Not at all."

"Will you eat someone I suggest?"

"But of course."

"Good. Joan has this coming. Let's visit her first." Winnie stepped into the red symbol and embraced the cold, primeval depravity. She felt sick as the shadow seeped into her very pores. She ran her tongue along her teeth, enjoying the feel of the canines for the first time in her life. She quivered, skin stretched and muscles inflexible, as though containing the extra being made movement difficult. The implanted neuron regulators responsible for emotional directive flared, blinding her. Her ears rang, her head ached, and her hands twisted into claws. She scratched her temple, seeking the implanted information-acquisition unit. Blood spurted over her nails.

The thing inside spoke, each word hammering. "What is this, here in your head?"

"It's how we learn. Information is loaded right into the unit."

The technology screeched. Winnie clutched her head. "Please stop! It hurts." Her knees gave way, and she pitched forward, vomiting.

The thing laughed. "This has no information about my kind. The royal non-royals have no way to stop me, since they don't believe I exist."

Winnie stretched toward the book, leaving streaks of blood to mark her passage.

"No you don't," it hissed. "I know your thoughts and intentions. You won't exorcise me. I think I like it here."

Winnie groaned, then fell silent.

A voice unlike her own escaped like corpse gas from her lips. "Let's make some princess pudding."

Aria in Black

Of all the colors in the world, Aria chose as her favorite a non-color. Black. Black like the kohl eyeliner she used to trace deep accents around her eyes. Black like the clothing of the Goth kids. Black like the uniform her father wore before he died.

Black comforted her. Night brought black, and in its shadowy folds, she wrote angry poetry. She cursed the eruption of stars that marred inky-dark skies with their glittering. Black was silent, solitary, cool, not cluttered with shining bits. Refined black needed no ostentation. In black she could lose inhibitions and be her true self.

However, Aria's Grandmother insisted she dress in the most hateful of colors. Pink.

Grandmother bought expensive garments and had them tailored to fit Aria's slim figure. She presented the latest purchase, a leather jacket died muted salmon with red accents.

"You must wear this." She held it out for Aria, unyielding until the girl punched her hands through the armholes. "It'll keep you warm these cold nights, Aria."

Aria backed away, arms crossed before her, and sighed. "Why pink, Grandmother? You know I don't like pink."

Grandmother reached for Aria's cheek with a hand that trembled with age. "Pink is for protection." Grandmother's gaze bored into Aria.

"Whatever." Aria stomped from the house and slammed the door. "Protection from what?" she asked the darkness. "Overprotective guardians?"

She hadn't walked long when someone stepped from the shadows of a tree. Bark-brown hair fell to thin shoulders. Aria couldn't tell the lithe person's gender. The voice floated like owl's wings, subdued and hushed as a secret.

"Hello. You're Aria, aren't you?"

Aria assumed a combative pose, legs bent and apart, weight balanced for blows or flight as needed. "How do you know that?"

The person shrugged. "Seen you around. Nice jacket."

Aria sneered. "You kidding me?"

"No."

"It's pink."

Pearly teeth reflected the streetlight as the person laughed. "And you don't like pink?"

Aria relaxed from combat-ready with the genial banter. "Hate it."

The person drew near and ran an appreciative hand along the lapel. "What's pink but a blend of blood and snow? Still, if it's holding you back, I'll take it off your hands." The person flipped hair out of eyes brilliant as moonlight. "I'd look good in that, don't you think?"

Aria nodded. "Yeah, you would. But why would I give it to you?"

A smirk crossed the elf-like features. "You don't like it. I do. You could say it got lost.

I'm sure your dear Grandmama will buy you another."

Aria stiffened. "Wait, I didn't tell you it was from my Grandmother."

"Sure you did. Don't you remember? When I first complimented you about it. You said she makes you wear pink even though you hate it."

Night air whistled around Aria's head like a migraine pressing on soft temples. "Oh, I guess I forgot." Heat boiled beneath her skin. She unzipped her jacket. "I don't think I should just give this to you, though."

"I can pay you." The person stepped into Aria's personal bubble which would usually distress Aria, but for some reason, Aria didn't mind the nearness. A biting blend of fresh-churned dirt and mown sweetgrass wafted between them. The person wrapped long-fingered hands about her waist. "I can pay you with a kiss."

Aria enjoyed the warmth of touch. The inches between their lips trembled like agony. Boy or girl, it didn't matter. Aria wanted to breathe in this first kiss, become lost in its moment and force it to last a lifetime.

A lick from a pink tongue across plump lips sent shivers racing up Aria's spine.

The owl-soft voice asked, "Would you like the kiss? It'll change your whole world."

Aria gasped shallow swallows of still, cool air, eyes locked on the prize. She would devour the kiss, cling to it like a soul lost in the depths of despair, rip it from those transfixing lips. She closed her eyes and nodded.

"Well then give me the jacket, Aria."

Aria struggled from the leather folds. It clung at her wrists like a parental warning. She turned the sleeves inside out in her haste to pull the jacket from her. As she slipped it into the other's grasp, their lips collided. Aria melted into the softness of the experience, warmth racing through her veins.

When they separated, Aria moaned at the interruption. The air shimmered with dark waves, like a shadow ocean washing all traces of color from the world. All color that is, except the spectacle before her.

Aria's kissing partner donned the jacket, slipping into it as easily as an eel gliding through murky waters. Its pink dye divided into blood spilled upon a snowdrift, unexpected as a first menses clotted upon pristine sheets. The being's brown hair bled into the collar of the jacket until it assumed the ruby and pearl hew. Its skin faded to bone-white, and crimson lips pulled back in mockery.

"Aria. Have I frightened you?" Its cruel laugh echoed like the swirl of decaying leaves.

Aria reeled and gasped as the night closed in on her. "Grandmother said to wear pink for protection."

"Protection, yes. But not protection for you." The being's throaty laughter left Aria weak and angry. "It's for protection from you." The person stepped into the tree's shadow, dripping garnet and frost upon the ground. "Dear sister, don't you understand? You must embrace what you are, as I've done. Red and white suits me, just as black suits you."

Ebony tinted Aria's skin, sept into her blood, settled in her heart, not the comforting embrace of awaiting dreams, but instead the hot, insatiable hunger of a nightmare.

The person reached toward a flickering street lamp, and it burst into a blinding flash of red and white. Its form grew insubstantial, incorporeal. Pink coalesced into suburban sidewalks, "Do Not Enter" signs, and the faded blossoms from forgotten spring times. It pooled in puddles reflecting childhood bedrooms and little girls' hair bows until it and the person and the jacket were no more.

With its departure, black enveloped Aria. It seeped into repressed crevices within her psyche. She drowned in its folds, cold, shaking, lonely. Within its suffocating embrace, she understood at last, realized her Grandmother's efforts. She recognized the fear concealed in neighbor's side-long glances. The panic bubbling beneath classmates' reluctant interactions. The misery in her Grandmother's responses.

Pink preserved innocence. Pink protected. It didn't protect Aria. It protected from her secret, dark nature.

Too late, Aria regretted her love of black.

Photo

Pauline swaddling her baby t_ght within the hand-knitted softness of a monogrammed blanket. The peachy fuzz atop his head promised darkness like his Daddy's hair, a promise time would hold hostage. With care, she raised his head and wrapped his baptismal rosary about his neck, holding her breath to avoid the lack of baby-freshness.

The photographer pointed to a metal and cloth apparatus. "Prop him here." The child's head lulled, and Pauline felt melancholy, but they posed, minute by motionless minute.

When reviewing the result, she asked, "Why are we blurred while the baby's clear?"

"Death provides the stillness photography requires."

Pierrot's Performance

Gaspard Pedrolino applied the white greasepaint without flaws as he did every day, defining him as the butt of pranks, the fool for love, Pierrot. The members of his Commedia del'Arte troupe called him by the sad clown's name, just as they referred to themselves as their alter-identities. Doctore, Pantelone, Il Capitano, and the hated Harlequin peddled bawdy, improvised *lazzis* while wearing elaborate masks. Pierrot, the Lovers, and the ladies, Rufianna, Vittoria and Columbine wore only make-up and costumes to define their parts.

His costume featured white clothes with white buttons, white ruff and white skull cap, white, the color of innocence, the color of skulls, the color of death.

Pierrot juggled, performed acrobatics, and danced. He pantomimed. He spoke with resignation, infrequent and halting. He hated his speech, the way his words slurred and stuttered. Silence best served him. Talking yielded unwanted ridicule.

He took his money and bought another treat for his beloved, Columbine. The woman's sparkling eyes reminded him of a night full of stars. Her pale skin shone like a full moon. Her hair fell in brown curls to her waist. Pierrot enjoyed brushing it for her, stroking it to rabbit-like softness. Her laugh tinkled like celestial music. He enjoyed lavishing her with gifts from trinkets to jewelry, cloths and favored meals. She accepted with charming curtseys and batted eyelashes. She often employed a fan to shield her face from a cherry-bright flush when he paid her court. He admired her modesty.

"My Pierrot, what have you brought for me this evening?" She placed a small hand on the full skirts gathered at her hip. He glimpsed her ankle. Heat rose beneath his face paint. He thrust a bouquet of snowy daisies given to him by a child who attended the performance.

"Flowers?" she cleared her throat, "Oh, fragrant offerings. Thank you." Her hips swayed as she walked to the tavern, singing a seaman's tune.

He longed to pinch the apples of her bottom, but he treated his Columbine as a Lady. The scent of roasting meat overpowered street smells of spent chamber pots, rotting vegetation, and mud. His stomach protested that although his eyes might feast, his body hungered.

Columbine turned and called, "Aren't you coming, Pierrot? The tavern keeper liked our performance. He said that we can eat there tonight."

They ate hearty lamb stew from trenchers of hard, dark bread set upon knotty, wooden tables. The tavern guests loomed close to participate in the troop's loud conversations filled with double entendres.

Capitano picked up a workman's bag. "Ah, I see you are a man who knows a good screw!" They all laughed.

"Indeed I do." The workman bought a round of ale.

"To truly know if that is so, we should ask his wife," said

Vittoria.

"Better to ask his mistress!" said Rufianna. More guffaws resounded.

Capitano put a gloved hand on the women's shoulders. "Our company is very good company, indeed." Without his mask to obscure his features, the lecherous smile and waggling eyebrows spoke of intent.

Pantelone threw an arm around the serving wench's small waist. He nestled close to her pronounced collarbone, saying, "Ah, me pretty lass." He turned his eyes to look down her top.

A local student raised his tankard. "To the night's players!"

Harlequin jumped onto the bench. "We be players for your pleasure!" He thrust his hips forward in a vulgar dance. The laughter grew louder in the stifling common room. Spirits of the patrons rose with the consumption of spirits.

Pierrot hunched over his food in a dark corner and watched. During performances, Pierrot stood apart from the rest, a sometimes harbinger of reason, a constant naive fool. The troop attracted loud conversations like dung collected flies. A local man whispered in Columbine's ear. She slapped him on his shoulder with a limp wrist, smiling. "Do you forget, Sir, that I am a Lady?"

Harlequin leapt to her side. "True of this one." He laughed. "But isn't it quaint ado about nothing?"

Columbine ducked her head behind her carved sandalwood fan. Harlequin cozied up on the bench between the townsman and Columbine, forcing the man to leave. She turned her face to Harlequin and he gazed into her eyes. He looked demure without his mask and motley robes, but shrewdness resided in his eyes.

Pierrot looked away, a shudder racing down his spine. The metal tankard scraped the table as he pushed it and his stew away. He felt sick. He exited without a word, making his way to their wagons and carts. Tears streaked his paint.

How could he get Columbine to love him as much as he loved her?

The cool night air dried his tears. His long strides took him to the camp where he started a fire. He washed his face and stretched out on a bed roll beneath the stars. A breeze played with the hair revealed when he removed the skull cap. He imagined it was Columbine's fingers.

A cloud moved, revealing a skeleton-pale moon. The moon, with its changeable nature, fascinated Pierrot. *So like my Columbine, unreachable, mysterious, and beautiful.*

"Moon, I love her," he confessed before sleep overtook him. In his dreams, Columbine nestled beside him and lavished gentle kisses on his cheeks and lips. He wished to remain lost in this illusion. However, he woke before the others and laid a simple breakfast for the troop.

What can I do to impress Columbine today?

He took a stroll.

In town, Pierrot negotiated with a goldsmith for a delicate ring fitted with a single, perfect garnet as dark as dried blood. Columbine would be enchanted by its exquisite craftsmanship, he felt certain.

He returned with his prize to camp. The players began to stir, but as the night involved carousing, several strangers straggled, shame-faced, from beds. Pierrot, unrecognizable without his defining attire, nodded but kept his eyes down-cast.

No point embarrassing them.

He sat oriented toward Columbine's resting place, as usual, tending the fire. He fingered the ring in his pouch. The circle of gold felt cool. It barely fit to the first knuckle on his littlest finger. Columbine's fingers, fine and lean, would look regal wearing his gift. He hoped she'd kiss his cheek as a thanks as she did in his dream last night.

He recalled first seeing Columbine when the troop of actors arrived in his village. The antics of the other players mattered little to him. His attention and affection focused on the grace of the girl playing the daughter, Columbine. His heart beat in time with her footfalls. His breathing grew dependent upon her laughter. Young, agile, and willing to learn, he offered his services as a player. He said goodbye to his old life and joined the troop. A wistful smile played at the corners of his lips.

Ah, Columbine.

Doctore and Capitano hunched over, as though shielding their eyes from the morning rays.

Vittoria elbowed Rufianna's ribs. Primal sounds came from Harlequin's tent.

"They've been at it all night!" said Vittoria.

"Yep, Harley has some stamina," said Rufianna.

"Who'd have guessed she'd be such a lusty wench?" asked Capitano. He stroked his mustache with deliberate, thoughtful movements.

Pierrot cast curious glances at Columbine's tent. *When's she getting up?*

Pantelone stumbled to collapse into a seat near the cook fire. He reeked of liquor. The couple in Harlequin's tent screamed with pleasure.

"Oh, still? They kept me up most of the night," he complained. He opened a flask and gulped the amber liquid. "Ah, that's better."

"Don't get too close to the fire, Pants, or you'll toast," Doctore chuckled.

Rustling from Harlequin's abode drew their attention. The players hooted when the woman emerged, flushed, hair in disarray, fastening her bodice over her copious bosom.

Pierrot stopped breathing. He felt weak. His breakfast threatened a reappearance. His peripheral vision closed in. Gasping, he stood. He trembled, disbelieving.

The troop focused on her.

"So, how did everything come out?" Vittoria sauntered to her friend.

The object of his undying affection colored and hid behind her unkempt hair.

Columbine. No. Please, no.

Unobserved, Pierrot dropped back. Anger crept into his heart like a snake. It coiled around his thoughts, squeezing them into a taunt, quivering rage. He glimpsed Harlequin on his bedroll, arms stretched behind his head. He wore a look of satisfaction and nothing more.

Columbine brushed passed him, tousle-haired head ducked.

She stunk of sex.

The improvisational actors joked and hooted. Pierrot turned from them to follow Columbine to her tent.

"Columbbbine."

She turned and looked up at him with brown eyes sunken behind dark, puffy circles. Her lips pinched into a thin line. His fingertip slipped into the gift.

"What is it, Pierrot?"

"I-I-I-I had ssssomething for you."

Her eye lids widened and her mouth relaxed. "Oh? You dear man! What is it?"

He pointed to her tent. She crossed her arms.

"I'm tired, Pierrot."

He nodded.

"I'll shshshow you in private."

She tapped a slippered foot, brow wrinkled in thought.

"Okay, but just for a minute." She led the way.

Inside, she said, "What do you have for me?"

He noticed yesterday's bouquet discarded and trampled in a corner.

Anger lent confidence to his speech. "Why did you gggo with him?"

She balled her hands into tight fists. "That is none of your business, but just so you know, he makes me laugh."

"I could make you laugh, too."

She threw back her head and guffawed. "You? Oh Pierrot," she rested a hand on his arm.

He narrowed his eyes, sensing her derision. A heaviness formed in his stomach. He clenched his jaw.

"You are our straight-man, not funny at all. Now what do you have for me? I need to get some sleep before our performance."

He grasped her hand and pulled her toward her bed. "What are you doing?" Her voice sounded frightened.

"You want to laugh." He pushed her onto the bed and pinned her with his body. He tickled her underarms and ribs, feeling the loosened stays of her corset. She pushed against his mass without effect. He reached behind his back to squeeze her thighs. She jumped and squealed.

"Stop," she chortled.

He continued. She squirmed to get away from his attention. He pulled her back.

Laugh. I can make you laugh.

He pushed harder with his fingertips. Tears streamed down his face as he imagined Columbine's nocturnal activity.

She gasped, struggling to escape his powerful grip. He tickled, bruising her. She thrashed. Her head fell off of the bedding. Unrelenting, he ministered to her sensitive skin. She stopped worming and lay still and silent.

His anger left him spent. She had laughed. He touched her.

Of course, so did Harlequin, and he didn't just tickle her.

He shook himself.

Don't think about that.

He stood over her. "Sssssee, I cccan mmmake you llllaugh." She did not acknowledge him, face turned away. He knelt beside her, taking her small, pale hand. "Ccccolumbbbine, fffor you." He slipped the ring onto her finger. It looked perfect. "IIII llllove yyyyyyyou." Tears coursed down his face.

She did not answer or look at the ring. She did not move.

"Ddddid yyyyou hhhear me, Ccccolumbbbine?"

Columbine remained still and silent.

He felt a cold dread creep down his spine and pool in his knees. "Ccccolumbbbbinnnne?"

Why didn't she acknowledge?

He rolled her over. Her eyes bulged, staring and unblinking. Her mouth gaped, tongue peeking, lips pale. Panting, he stumbled away from the lifeless woman.

I only tickled her.

No breath betrayed her chest. No movement flickered with a sign of life.

Is it even possible to tickle somebody to death?

A scream gurgled in his throat, but he strangled it down.

Nobody will recognize me without my makeup.

He threw up in the corner atop the discarded bouquet.

Columbine, forgive me.

He said goodbye to Pierrot and ran.

Where Once Flourished

They wormed their way into her brain, the words the bullies said. They hollowed out places within her confidence until, honeycombed with doubt, she shook with indecision. Leeches who sucked her passions until, bloated and flush with their victory, they moved on to new prey. Ironically, they gained nothing of value, but they left a hollowed shell behind where once flourished a beautiful and artistic spirit.

Pillow Talk

Timmy shuffled into the living room. He ran a chubby hand through disheveled hair and rubbed his puffy eyes. With a yawn, he said, "I can't sleep, Momma."

Sheila looked up from her novel with a sigh. "For goodness sakes, why on earth not?"

Timmy leaned his head on the arm of his mother's overstuffed chair. "The little girl won't stop talking."

"What little girl, Timmy?"

"The one from the trees."

She closed the book with a thud of parental resolve, then grasped his hand and marched him into his bedroom. She pointed to the bed.

"Climb in." She tucked the soft blanket over his shoulder and sat beside him on his bed. "Sweetheart, you don't need to be afraid of the dark. This is your room. You are safe here."

"But Momma, she lives here too."

"You, my dear, have such an active imagination." She ruffled his hair, then walked around the room. "Is the girl here now?"

"I don't see her."

She opened the door to the closet and stepped inside. "Nobody here." She lifted the dust ruffle. "Nobody here, either." She pulled aside the curtains. "Your room appears to be little girl free." She kissed his forehead. "Now get some sleep, my love."

He wriggled deeper under the covers. The pillow cradled his head. She leaned over, kissed him, and turned off the light. "I'll leave your nightlight on and the door open. I'll be just down the hall. Now get some sleep."

She resumed her comfortable position in her chair and opened her book, but the words swam before her eyes. *I'm too tired to read.* She closed her eyes and settled into the cushion. The floating pre-sleep tingled over her when a strange sound brought her to attention.

"Get up now. Let's play."

"I want to sleep. Leave me alone. Please."

"Get up, boy."

"My Momma's going to be mad."

She stiffened, unnerved. The voices sounded distinct and differentiated, Timmy and someone else. "What the heck?" She wondered as she crept down the hall. She peeked around the corner into her son's room. He sat up in bed, hugging his teddy bear to his chest.

"Please, Momma, make her stop. I'm tired."

She flipped on the light and searched. "Where is she?"

"I don't know. She left right before you came in."

Nowhere else to hide. She shivered. *Gosh, it's cold in here.* She thrust her hands into the deep front pockets of her robe and chewed the inside of her cheek. She cleared her throat and said in a stern voice, "Okay, here's the deal. This room belongs to Timmy. Do not bother him. No talking. He needs to sleep."

Timmy tugged the sleeve of her robe. The circles under his eyes darkened in the shadows like bruises. He whispered, "She's not going to like it, Momma. She can't sleep, so she doesn't want me to, either."

She bent and kissed her son, then sat on the floor beside his bed and stroked his hair until he dozed off. With the door ajar, the temperature warmed. Once she heard his gentle snore, she left to claim her own bed.

As she settled into the soft support of the pillow, body relaxing into the mattress, a sound froze her in place. Muscles rigid, ears pricked to hear the slightest sound, she scanned the room. *Nothing there.* She shivered but snuggled deeper into the comforter and calmed her heart rate. Her eyes slid shut.

Her knees locked up. *What's that? A child's voice?*

"That wasn't very nice. I can't sleep. Why should he?" The whine grated. "Now who will I talk to? Guess I'll talk to you instead."

She kept her eyes sealed tight. *Be reasonable. The kid's playing a weird game's all.* "Timmy, this is not funny, young man." *How's he changing his voice like that? He really sounds like a girl.*

"I'm not Timmy."

No way. This has got to be my imagination.

She cracked her eye open, like opening a sigil on a tomb. The dim gloom from the streetlight revealed the child beside her bed, about the same size as Timmy.

The high-pitched voice took a deeper resonance. "If I can't sleep, why should you? Why should he?"

Sheila felt a chill and pulled the covers tighter about her body.

"This is no longer funny. Go to bed now!"

"I would! I want to sleep! I can't! I haven't slept since they left me here, all alone. I'm so tired, but I can't sleep! I'm so cold." The outburst ended with sloppy sobs.

Sheila reached to pull the child into her arms, to wrap the confusion and cold with a warm blanket and love. "Come here, honey. Come here and rest. Please, I don't understand. It must be a bad dream or something you saw on television. I'm here. You're not alone."

Sheila's teeth chattered, and her body quaked with cold. The child remained just outside of her grip. She sat up and stretched toward the sobbing child.

"But I am alone! You don't understand. Poppa and Momma left me, said I was too sick to make the trip, just left me under the trees." The child shook with hiccups.

What kind of game is this? Sheila's bedroom door opened, flooding the room with light from the hallway. Timmy stood in the doorway rubbed both fists over his eyes. "Momma, sorry, but I still can't sleep."

Sheila jumped back into her bed, recoiling from the cold, numb with disbelief. She stared at her son illuminated on the threshold, mouth slack and then turned, wooden with shock, to behold the face of her conversation with death

Pleased as Punch

The couple embraced, wooden, smiles painted across frozen faces.

"I have some errands to run. Please babysit," Judy said.

"Of course," he said, tinny voice reminiscent of a kazoo. The smile hid his displeasure.

Judy kissed her husband and son, then collected her purse and left, humming.

Father and boy regarded each other without blinking. The child's lower lip jutted, quivered, and then stretched into a wide "O." His shrill scream accosted Punch's sensitive ears. He covered them with trembling hands.

"Oh, stop that caterwauling," he yelled. The baby's cries intensified.

Punch picked up the baby and held him at an angle, bouncing him until the child's head bobbed. The baby's shrieks bounded in time. The little face reddened and tears coursed unchecked over his scrunched-up face.

"Noisy, noisy, noisy," Punch sing-songed, ignoring the child's distress. "Just like your mother. She's never quiet, either." He turned the child. He regarded him, father's pointy nose pressed against the child's upturned. "I could give you something to cry about!"

A knock on the back door drew Punch's attention. He set the

crying child in his wooden cradle. Before opening the door, he adjusted his colorful, motley-patterned robe.

On the step, a buxom woman stood, shuffling her feet. He greeted her with an embrace. "Pretty Polly, my own dear girl!"

Polly stepped into the kitchen to fall into his embrace. "I saw her leave," she breathed as he lavished kisses on her rosy cheeks and slender neck. Punch slipped his arms out of his robe and pulled her to his naked chest. She gasped, and he caressed the exposed tops of her breasts.

"Stop, stop, please Punch! I can't."

"Yes, you can. You always do."

"Not with that baby crying."

"What?"

"I can't with that baby crying."

Stupid baby.

"I'll shut him up. Wait right here."

Punch looked at the infant whose wadded fists and padded feet struck at the air. The salty smell of soiled diaper permeated the room.

"Stop it, you little bastard!" he hissed. "That's it, isn't it? You are a bastard, not mine at all. If you were mine, you would love me. You would want to be with me. You would want me to be happy."

He grasped the baby by the arms, disregarding his lolling head. "Polly is waiting to make me happy, but you have to shut up!" He shook the baby into stunned silence. "That's better." He plunked the staring child onto the elephant-decorated cotton cradle sheet and rejoined Polly.

He lifted her onto the kitchen table and hiked up her skirts. "Pant for me, Polly."

Judy's chicken noodle soup simmered on the stove while the lovers collapsed onto each other.

"I'd better go before your wife gets home."

"I suppose." He slapped her bottom as she left.

None too soon. His grin turned lecherous.

The hinges of the front door squealed in protest as Judy returned home. She deposited four paper grocery bags on the wooden kitchen table. She nodded a greeting to her husband who leaned on the kitchen door frame wearing only his briefs and his favorite tasseled sugarloaf hat.

"Give you any ideas?" he wagged his arched eyebrows toward his receding hairline.

"Let me check on the baby, and then I might just."

"He's quiet. Come here." Punch pointed to the blue tile on the floor directly in front of him.

She shook her head. "I'll just check on him first."

She paused midstride when he yelled, "I said get over here, woman. I don't mean when you feel like it. I mean now."

She stiffened, glaring at him through narrowed eyes, then walked into the living room.

He closed his eyes. He felt Polly around him still.

Judy's scream ripped through his reverie.

She ran into the kitchen, clutching the baby, hysterical.

Punch looked at her, eyes wide with wonder.

"You aren't making any sense. Calm down."

"I can't calm down. He isn't waking! Oh my God, what happened to him?"

His hand met her cheek before he realized he planned to strike. Her face bore an angry imprint from the contact.

She backed away.

"Judy, he must have SIDS."

"SIDS? Do you mean Sudden Infant Death Syndrome?"

"Yeah, that's it."

She clutched the child to her shoulder, backing away from her husband.

"Why did you hit me?"

"You were going crazy. I had to calm you down."

"Of course I am going crazy! There is something wrong with the baby!"

She reached into her hip pocket for her cellular telephone and dialed 911.

"What are you doing? Judy, hang up."

"I'm calling an ambulance."

"What for?"

She stared at him as though he were crazy.

"Please send an ambulance to 1662 Covent Garden Court."

He slapped the phone from her hand. It shattered as it hit the floor.

"What is wrong with you?"

"Why would you call an ambulance if the brat is already dead?"

She stared, wide-eyed, and backed away.

How dare she act like there was something wrong with him? He'd knock that look right off her face.

He grabbed a wooden stick that he kept near the kitchen door to frighten away the neighbor's cat. Judy yelled and pleaded while Punch cackled. The ruckus did not stop until a pounding sounded at the front door.

"Pull yourself together," Punch hissed at his weeping wife. Judy huddled in the corner, her hunched body sheltering the baby.

"What can I do for you, officer?" Punch squawked.

"There is a reported domestic dispute in progress. May I speak to your wife, please?"

Punch pushed the heels of his hands into his bulging eyes, his ever-present smile clownish. "I'm sorry. She's not here."

"Mr. Punch, isn't it? I must insist I talk with her."

Punch bore his teeth, his grip tightening on his concealed slapstick. He raised his voice to alert Judy. "I told you, she ain't here."

She better stay hidden.

She didn't.

Bruised, hair disheveled, makeup streaming down her face, she limped into the living room cradling the silent child. Her sniffling sickened him.

Can't follow the simplest of instructions.

"Ah, there you are, my pet!" Punch trilled in a falsetto. She flinched when he approached.

"Ma'am, are you alright?" The officer's tone put him on alert. *Was this encounter pre-meditated?*

Punch wheeled on the uniformed man, the blow taking him by

surprise. A sickening crack resonated as the stick hit the officer before he hit the wooden floor with a thud. His blue hat spiraled. Judy opened her mouth in a silent scream, her face transformed in terror.

"Now, honey, let's work this out," Punch simpered.

Judy reached a shaking hand toward him but backed away.

Punch raised his bloodied stick like a batter about to hit the game-winning home run. Judy ran. He heard the kitchen screen door slam marking her retreat. He pursued.

As he exited, he felt a heavy blow, saw stars. His slapstick flew from his hands, skittered across the uncut lawn.

Judy's falling down on her duties. The place looks a mess.

Another blow. He turned his head to see Judy, still cradling the child, swinging a tree limb at his head. Sirens screamed. Stars erupted like an Independence Day celebration, and then Punch lost consciousness.

When he came to, Punch's head ached. It nauseated him to move.

Where am I?

His arms bent unmovably behind his back. He sat on the molded plastic seat in the back of a squad car. He recognized the driver as the officer who came to his house earlier. The man's head bore white bandages. Punch felt blood clumping in his hair and oozing to saturate his collar.

"Don't I get medical treatment?" he demanded.

"You get booked first."

Big man with the gun, huh?

"Booked for what?"

"Assault against an officer. Assault against your wife. Assault against a minor. If that baby dies, the charges will change." The officer lifted his chin to glare in the rearview mirror at Punch. "Lots of wives don't press charges. Yours is. You're going away for a long, long time, little man." He touched the back of his head. "You better get a good attorney."

A voice drew his attention. Beside him in the back of the squad car, Punch saw his defense in a man with red skin, black hair and goatee, and horns sprouting from his head.

"Poor Punch. It's not like you ground the brat up to make sausage or fed it to a crocodile," this apparition laughed. The officer showed no sign of hearing the devil's voice. Punch's manic grin never left his face.

Haiku 4

Rage manifested

Justice's thundered tempest

Wrongs would be made right

What the
Accident Took

Headaches, echoes of what brought me to this twilight half-world of monitors, fluorescent lighting, and needles. Taped wires trap my arm.

I push covers and gasp.

"No," I groan. My nightdress slumps unimpeded.

No thick thighs or twist-prone ankles.

I stare, horrified. I reach. No legs.

Pledging Amaris

Ulrich bounded after the raven-haired woman while balancing a cardboard cup puffing fragrant coffee steam from the sip cap. "Hey, Lucy! Wait up!"

Something about Lucy made Ulrich trust her. Sure, pretty described and defined her, with her long, flowing hair and mysterious Spanish eyes, but her personality drew him like a siren song.

She turned, a nebulous smile stretched across her pale feature.

He stretched out the coffee, struggling to keep his panting voice even. "Just the way you like it."

She accepted the cup and sniffed. "Perfect. How'd you know I needed some caffeine?"

He ignored the stitch in his side and laughed. "You said you're more nocturnal." The mischievous glint in her eye sent a thrill racing up his spine. "Now, how are you going to carry your books and balance your coffee?" He took her books. "Please, let me help."

He shivered at her throaty laugh. "But my classes are clear across campus, while yours are right there." She nodded toward his freshman classrooms.

"True, but what sort of gentleman leaves a lady in such distress? Please let me." He loved watching her lips caress the edge of the cup.

With a slight inclination of her head, he took up the burden and followed. Her jazz-singer's alto soothed as they discussed her upcoming astronomy class. When he worked up the nerve to ask her on an actual date, the resulting earthquake from her laughter threatened to wreck his insides. "Ulrich, don't you know I only date a certain type of person?"

"What type of man, Lucy?"

Her lids shaded eyes like clouds covering the moon. "It's sort of a fraternity/little sister thing. I can only date people in Amaris."

"What's Amaris?"

Her smile stretched to reveal a dazzling smile. "It's an exclusive club." She nodded toward gray stone buildings situated to the west. "Been on this campus since the school started."

He straightened to his greatest height. "Well, can I join?"

Her smile held secrets he wanted to collect as kisses. "You can try. I don't know how hard it would be on you, though. Pledging and hazing and all."

He pointed to his puffed out chest. "Sign me up."

"You'd do that for me? I hear it's a lot of work and a difficult transition."

He leaned closer, enjoying her scent. Like rain. "I'd do anything for you."

She brought him to a party and introduced him to some members, including Randal. "He's interested in joining."

Randal, a well-dressed senior in the engineering program, gave him a critical eyeballing as he drank red wine from a crystal glass. He licked a trace of red from his lips. "Are you, now? What brings you to Amaris?"

Ulrich glanced at Lucy's retreating form. She seemed to glow in the dim crowd, as though a spotlight followed her every move.

Randal followed Ulrich's gaze. "Ah, Lucy. She brings us all here, actually, but we don't always realize it." He took a final swallow from his glass. "Guess that puts you a bit ahead of the curve." He scowled at his empty glass. "You a freshman?"

Ulrich nodded and extended his hand. "Second semester. Can I get you a refill?"

Randal's lips curved upward, revealing dazzling white teeth. "Yes, Pledge. You can."

Pledge? Ulrich fought against running to the bar in his eagerness to impress Randal. When he returned the fresh glass to its owner, he met other members of Amaris. They all seemed intent on keeping Ulrich busy with menial tasks.

After the party, Ulrich filled his days with studies and coffee with Lucy. Amaris occupied his evenings. He scrubbed out the houses after parties, ran errands, and cleaned laundry. He made household silver shine and memorized the names of all the members before him. Amaris revealed secrets with its members. Ulrich intended to prove his worthiness and learn all Amaris had to share.

One afternoon, a boy of about ten knocked on Ulrich's door. Dressed in anachronistic livery like a royal footman, he bowed and presented a letter on a silver platter. Ulrich's snort of laughter caused the boy to frown, but he remained stiff and composed. After Ulrich retrieved the letter, the boy turned and marched away with the exaggerated gait of a miniature soldier.

Hand calligraphy on heavy, linen stationery invited him to a moonlight Amaris soirée, white tie required. Ulrich leapt into the air, whooping with excitement, before he scrambled to rent a tuxedo, shoes, and gloves. On impulse, he splurged on moonstone cufflinks and a snowy silk kerchief. The shopkeeper assured him he looked the part of a success as he departed for the party.

As instructed, he arrived at the main house before the moon rose. The ancient stone building stood stark as a massive mausoleum in the twilight.

Despite the warm temperature, he shivered. *Wonder if they'll accept me as a member?*

Music from a string quartet floated on night air laced with the perfume of lupine and jasmine. He cleared his throat before knocking on the heavy oak door. Members of Amaris welcomed him in, sharp-toothed smiles stretched wide beneath glittering animal half-masks.

Ulrich gravitated to a tall man who seemed to command the room. He leaned to whisper, "I didn't know about the masks. Where can I get one?"

Randal's voice rumbled like a growl. "You'll earn one this evening, friend." He clapped Ulrich on the back and guided him to the bar where eight women in silver gowns dispensed goblets of dark spiced wine. "Your wish is about to come true."

Ulrich accepted a goblet from a graceful hand. The warm wine coated the glass and burned his throat as he swallowed. Randal tapped his glass, and the music stopped. "Attention, please. The man of the hour has arrived. He's completed our tasks and learned of our pedigree. Our own Lucy vouches for him."

One of the ladies in silver inclined her head and raised her glass.

"Ulrich, does your desire to become one of us remain unaltered?"

Ulrich's wispy mustache twitched, but his voice carried throughout the room. "It is my dearest wish to be a part of Amaris."

The masked assembly cheered and toasted with blood-red wine. Randal clapped gloved hands, dull thud after dull thud. "Ulrich shall learn our secrets. It is time."

A member stepped forward with a mask in hand. "You've earned this." In his gloved hands rested a wooly face. When he donned it, Ulrich could not see well through the eye holes, but he felt a part of the group. People shook his hand and thumped his back with hearty congratulations.

The women opened French doors leading to the veranda. The group surged around Ulrich, sweeping him along as they funneled outside. Ulrich stood in the center of a pack of well-dressed, masked people.

The women intoned, "Behold, the moon rises." Full and bright, the lunar beauty bloomed overhead and awed Ulrich.

"No wonder poets sing your praises, oh Diana," he whispered.

Warmth spread through him. Never in his life had he felt more contented. He'd worked himself to exhaustion seeking their favor, and this party proved his effort worthwhile. He smiled at Randal.

Randal's grin widened. His grip on Ulrich's collar tightened. "You did it, my friend. You're about to be one of us."

Tuxedoed bodies jostled with restless energy. Their jovial

laughter grew sinister. Grins elongated, and musky smells of kennels and locker rooms gagged Ulrich. He circled, but the wall of bodies trapped him.

"Little bites," one of the women said. *Was it his Lucy*? They looked alike in their ridiculous masks. *Wait! Bites*?

Glistening white fur captured moonlight. Pronounced snouts and shark-strong teeth closed in on him like a nightmare. "No!" he yelled, thrusting against the assailants.

"Don't fight it, Ulrich," a woman said, her sultry voice rising over the snarls of the men. "In the end, you'll have your wish."

He flailed against nips. Scratches dug through fabric and bit into his flesh. During the struggle, his kerchief fluttered to the ground, garnet splashes upon snow. He kicked and punched, but teeth punctured and tore. He collapsed to his knees, head light from blood loss, vision ebbing and flowing like the tide. The moonstone cufflinks indented into his flaming cheeks, unyielding pebbles. He heaved and vomited wine and bile.

The men backed away, pacing and restless, and women formed a circle around him, clasping hands like playground children. They swayed and danced, blinding pillars reaching to the night sky. He blocked the view with bloodied fists, but a sound rattled him. Howling. From every direction, howling echoed.

When he opened his eyes, he found himself mask-less and alone on the veranda. Party sounds inside drew his attention. He peered through a window. Members of Amaris mingled over cocktails and sampled *canapes* from waiters' trays. No masks. Impeccable dress clothes spot-free.

His own wrinkled formal-wear bore no bloody marks. *Did I dream it all? Black out after the wine?* He ran a shaking hand through wiry hair. His muscles ached with the movement. His cufflinks were missing. A glint in the bushes reflected the moonlight. Moonstone cufflinks snagged in hawthorn branches bore splashes of crimson.

Smells of roasted meat drew his attention. He stiffened at every shuffling, leather-clad foot inside as well as the hidden scampering of night creatures in the tall grasses at the property's edge.

Lucy opened the door and smiled, radiant in her floor-length white gown. "Are you feeling better? You looked a bit flushed." She extended a glass of wine with a gloved hand. He hesitated before accepting.

She raised her glass. "Congratulations, Ulrich. You're a member now." Luscious lips caressed the rim of the glass. He sipped his own, entranced by the sight. Her tongue darted to collect a stray droplet. "You have to come inside now. There's a new pledge you must meet."

He followed her inside, helpless as the tide beneath the ministrations of the moon. His cologne did little to disguise a growing musk, and he wrinkled his nose with displeasure.

A wide-eyed first year filled glasses and collected plates of hors d' oeuvres for members, including him. The young man averted his gaze as he presented Ulrich with a drink. The pledge nodded toward Lucy, beautiful with a secretive smile clouding her face. "She said this is the Amaris specialty drink. It's called the Wolf Pack."

She tipped her head, her hair cascading over her shoulders, and pursed her lips in imitation of a howl.

Ulrich's teeth crowded his lips, and he smiled. He patted the pledge's shoulder. The freshman cringed away from the contact like a sheep from a dog's bark.

Ulrich asked, "What makes you want to pledge Amaris?"

The young man's glance sidled to Lucy, and he blushed.

Ulrich nodded. "She brings us all here, I think."

The young man hurried away to wipe a spill. Ulrich heard the agitation of his heartbeat and longed to taste the young man's flesh. *Soon. A month at most, after he's done pledging.*

Haiku 5

Overwhelming foe

Wraps darkness as an embrace

Cloaked anxiety

Ringing Spirits

Mandy's feet wobbled on sparkling designer heels. Emotionally, she felt as unsteady as her gait. The door before her gleamed a brilliant white in the afternoon sun. She ran her hand through her thick hair and gulped before knocking.

"Hi! You must be Mandy. I'm Theresa." The shorter, middle-aged woman who opened the door stood steady in her heels. She extended a hand decorated with emerald and diamond rings and pampered with a French manicure. Her smile revealed perfect teeth and brightened her pale eyes.

Mandy shook hands and stepped inside through a hallway to a sitting room.

"Please, make yourself comfortable." Theresa indicated the seating options with a wave. Mandy sat on an overstuffed chintz chair. Theresa sat opposite her guest in a blue wingback.

"You know what I do. I talk with spirits."

Mandy nodded.

"You are surrounded by spirits. Let's start, shall we?"

Mandy shifted in her seat but maintained eye-contact. Theresa tapped her long fingernails on the side table. "Who is the female who passed whose name starts with an "S"?"

Mandy's head thrust into the chair back. She inhaled with a quick hiss. "um, I'm not sure."

The medium narrowed her eyes. "We'll come back to her, then.

Your dad is passed, right?"

Mandy nodded.

"He called you his princess." Mandy removed a handkerchief from her purse and wiped her eyes. A waft of floral perfume puffed out. Half-moons of black mascara marked the linen.

She sniffed a breathy, "Yeah."

"He is showing me a football. Does that mean something to you?"

Mandy flashed a small smile, like a minnow flashing silver in a stream. "He taught me to throw and catch."

"Well, he's telling you to keep throwing spirals." The women locked eyes in mutual appraisal. "He is also showing me a lake at sunrise and a boat."

Mandy's private laugh shook. "Yeah, we fished together, too."

"He is telling me, 'Man, Theresa, you should'a seen that kid bait a hook!'" Her voice quieted as she added, "He is proud of all that you accomplished. He says, 'Don't forget to remove the pin bones before cooking the trout.'"

Theresa's brow creased. "The woman with the "S" wishes to be acknowledged."

Mandy clutched her purse to her chest with both hands. "I told you, I don't know who that would be. Do you hear from my Grandmother or my sister?"

Head cocked, considering, Theresa nodded. "They are here. They say that they are always with you and love you. Your sister shows me a doll with long, red braids."

Mandy's hands flew to her lips, smudging a bit of her peach

lipstick on the kerchief. Her engagement and wedding rings glinted gold in the low light. "Oh my gosh! I still have the doll!"

"Does the name 'Katie' mean anything to you?"

"Yes, yes! That was the doll's name." Mandy's tears spilled unchecked over her flushed, prominent cheekbones, reflecting light like the diamond in her engagement ring.

"Were you recently married?"

Vigorous shaking sent the salty droplets from her face.

"Your mother or a mother figure walked you down the aisle?"

"Oh, wow! Yep, my mom did. How can you know that?"

"Please know your sister and father were there with you in spirit. Your father is glad that his wife filled the role he could not."

"I missed them so much!" Mandy sniffed.

"They are holding out white roses, which is their way of saying that they are with you, that they were there at your wedding and love you."

Theresa gazed to the left toward a candle flickering a cinnamon glow. She raised her hand to her chin, tapped with impatient fingers. Gypsy bangle bracelets sounded like wind chimes as they fell to her elbow. She shook her head.

"I am sorry, Mandy, but this woman with the 'S' is relentless. She is wearing a wedding dress and pointing at the roses. She's pushed your family back until you acknowledge her. Do you have any idea who she is?"

"Why is she pushing my family away? Please make her stop."

"She is showing me a young girl with dark hair like hers. You cut this little girl's hair."

Mandy sat rigid and upright, as though frozen by the sudden drop in temperature.

Theresa's breath puffed out as she said, "She wants you to give back her jewelry."

"I, I don't have any of her jewelry!"

The lights flickered.

"Do you have a child?"

"I have a step-daughter, Sammy."

"Sammy?" A smell of cigarette smoke drifted through the room, and both women shivered. "Is Sammy your current husband's daughter?"

"Yes."

Theresa's face became animated while she worked out her next question.

"And Sammy's mother is with the spirits?"

"My husband is a widower, yes."

The smell of burning grew more intense. Theresa cleared her throat. "What is his deceased wife's name?"

"Why?"

"Do you know her name?"

Mandy considered before answering. "Her name is Samantha. Sammy is named after her mother."

"Okay," Theresa's points her palms toward her client, like a traffic cop demanding compliance. "Samantha is definitely here with a message. She does not like you holding on to what she feels belongs to her daughter."

Mandy felt sick to her stomach. A ringing in her ears made

concentrating difficult. Shaking her head in denial did not clarify her thoughts. She licked her lips, then the waterworks began with renewed quivering.

"But I don't have anything of hers." She sobbed.

The lights blinked. The street noise no longer infiltrated their room, lending a parlor-like quality to the space.

"Is she haunting us? Is she angry that I married Jackson?"

Theresa inhaled, her buxom chest rising. She closed her eyes, then leveled a look like cold, blue diamonds boring into her client.

"What did you do with her possessions?"

"Jackson took care of that. He gave away the clothing to charity. The collectibles and jewelry are Sammy's now."

"All of it? Samantha seems to believe you are in possession of something important to her."

The crying intensified. Mandy rocked in her seat, begging, "Please, I don't know what it could be! Please ask her to leave us alone." She wiped moisture and makeup with shaking hands, confusing tears with the engagement solitaire.

Theresa grabbed Mandy's cold, trembling hands in hers. "Relax, please. I need you to think. Did your husband give you any jewelry?'

"Just our wedding set. He designed it himself." She regarded her left hand. The Diamond blinked like a venomous reptile.

Theresa touched a finger to the stone, then fell back with a strangled gasp. She convulsed.

Mandy gasped. "Theresa, are you okay?"

The medium's eyes rolled into her head. "Jackson designed

your engagement set using a gem that he created from my ashes," came an otherworldly voice emanating from Theresa's still lips.

Mandy screamed. She backed away from the possessed woman, knocking chairs over in her haste. She removed her wedding ensemble, threw it on a marble curiosity table near the door, and she ran out to confront her husband.

Haiku 6

Power grows within

Hidden by frail forms and smiles

Poison in a kiss

Summoning War

"Don't worry, I've done lots of research! I've watched all the shows, and Wiki gave me the summoning spell," Jeremy said with confidence, adding ironically, "What could possibly go wrong?"

The group smiled with anticipation. They felt certain the experiences they'd amassed vicariously from the silver screen and television shows would arm and protect them. Several of the group even read a book or two on the subject, and they all were experienced gamers.

With care, they drew a circle of salt, ignited a bundle of sage using a pink lighter, and recreated the archaic symbols found from various sources. They together intoned ancient words invoking protection.

Bobbie could barely stifle a childish giggle. He felt nervous despite his proclaimed disbelief in "the project" as the group called it. Tom set up video cameras and recording devises throughout the room to capture every angle of the scene, intent on capturing for reality television an actual summoned spirit.

Jenna pursed her lips in a superior sort of way. She proclaimed herself "a sensitive." "I am more in tune with the spirit world than the average person," she explained. "This is laughable," she complained as an aside to Bobbie.

"Then why are you here?" he asked, unwrapping a packet of peanuts. He threw the sleeve of legumes into his mouth and chewed.

"I've got nothing else tonight," she shrugged. "My class work's all caught up and I've nowhere else to go."

"The sacred space is prepared. Now we must decide who we will summon," said Niles in a too-serious voice that made it hard for Chris and even harder for Bobbie not to devolve into giggles. Silence fell. The group breathed in the burnt sage and admired the ambience of the moment.

The six of them thus set up what in their estimation was a really cool summoning chamber in the basement of their dorm house. The basement of Eastern College gave the right dungeon-like feel, the cobwebs and their spiders adding a touch of Halloween-like ambience. Candles added enough light by which to see, reflecting the awaiting symbols transcribed onto the cement floor. The sounds from the other dormitory residents, uninvolved students going about their evening unaware of the ritual being conducted below their feet, echoed like ghostly warnings throughout the space.

"Spirit of the college that haunts this dormitory," began Chris, imitating the quavering "Poltergeist" movie medium as best she could, but she stopped when she saw the disapproval on the faces of the others.

"Dude, we need to know the name, or we won't have control over the creature," said Jeremy, trying to sound reasonable.

"I'm not a dude," Chris grumbled under her breath, "not that you'd notice."

Niles produced from his backpack a list of names. He had downloaded them from on-line esoteric sites. Everyone gathered around to share in the selection. "These are, like, demon names and stuff," said Tom, disappointed. "I thought that we were going to try to talk to a ghost."

Jenna nodded her manga-styled head, sharing Tom's disappointment.

"Cool!" said Bobbie, wearing a brave mask to disguise his discomfort. He was not going to allow his fears of the occult to interfere with inclusion in this group, since they were the only ones who seemed to not mind him being around. Though, in truth, Bobbie would have been much more comfortable eating a bag of Cheetos while resuming a role-playing or live-action computer game than standing here in this dank reminder of a B horror movie set. "Let's call Ares!" he said with bravado.

"Aries is an astrological symbol," said Jenna, sounding superior. "It is not a demon."

"I'm Aries!" said Chris, adding, "and so is Jeremy!" She smiled shyly at him, hiding the embarrassed flush that betrayed her crush behind her mousy, shoulder-length brown hair. Jeremy pretended not to notice Chris' attention or observation, focusing instead on the list of names, double spaced, printed on resume paper.

He sighed, bestowing indulgent smiles on the ladies. He fidgeted with his glasses as he pointed out, with an almost British, subtly assumed accent, "Ares was the name of the Greek god of war, also called Mars by the Romans."

Not to be outdone, Jeremy pointed out, "Many believed the ancient personifications were actually demons who walked among the humans. When you know their names, though, you can control them." He sounded smug. He crossed his arms and leveled them all with a look over his own wire glass rims.

"Great," said Bobbie in a high-pitched voice, his chubby face made rounder by his over-bright smile, adding, "let's call him then!"

"Call the god of war?" asked Jenna, condescendingly, "and what? Ask him for tea?"

Bobbie was cowed, by Jeremy and Niles rallied to his defense. "No, we could ask him to do anything we wanted. He could end the conflict in the Middle East," said Jeremy. Niles adding, "Reclaim the Holy Land." The two smiled tightly, united in their resolve.

"Imagine the knowledge that he could share with us!" gloried Tom, shifting his personal emphasis in the project.

Jenna, observing the lust for power in the boys' eyes, felt a resonance. She imagined what she would do if she were in charge of this summoned energy. She and Bobbie both knew that if they were given charge over such a powerful being, they themselves would become powerful. Then everyone would be forced to not only acknowledge, but also to kneel before them. No more ignoring or bullying. They would be powerfully backed people.

Chris went along with the rest, unconvinced.

All but Tom took places along the outside edge of the elaborate circle at the points of the detailed pentagram. After first activating the other recording devices, Tom manned his favorite video camera in a corner furthest from the door. The group intoned the ritual words earnestly, passionately, each attempting to outdo the other with zealousness. They spoke as they imagined they should, with sincerity and intent, their words blending with the smoke of the candles and the sage smudge bowls.

The air became possessed of a desperate cold which sent the electronics into a frenzy. Tom rushed to repair, but he was confounded. All of the equipment was failing. He froze, wondering if this could really be a supernatural occurrence. He scrambled to make even one of the dozen or so recording devises cooperate as the rest of the group swayed and intoned, no longer aware of Tom or their surroundings, caught in a frenzy that escalated to an ecstasy.

A stink of sulfur, a fog that could be from the hazy eyes, smoke, and bright flashes of light overwhelmed the room. Then there stood before the circle of would be demonologists a middle-aged man. He was not tall, but stocky, broad of shoulders, thick of legs. His wide, short-fingered hands bore several rings and held a red wooden walking stick. He took in his surroundings with eyes like those of a big cat, dark with glints of gold. Broad of face, with a classic Greek profile, strong chin, and tight brown curls cut short against his head, he stood nonchalantly.

Tom gasped, forgetting for the moment his equipment. The others shook to clear their heads and looked around.

"Holy shit!" yelped Jeremy, the first to recognize that a stranger stood in their presence, scrambling back. His mind reasoned that this was no supernatural threat but wondered how a professor had entered the room without them realizing it. His fear of expulsion from his academic pursuits became overwhelming. He ran from the room to disavow any knowledge of the night's activities. Thereafter, his intellect was addled, and he became crazed with regret for not standing to master the situation as was his self-prescribed destiny. Although through his charisma he was able to garner attention as a metaphysical "master," most who met him thought Jeremy mad. He could never recreate a summoning project.

Bobbie raced behind him, his mind filled with visions of raining fire and holy retribution. He would not associate with the others again, but instead transfer to another, better school, despite his substandard grades, where his wealthy family would secure for him a degree and a plush position at his Uncle James' arms company. Bobbie, in his later years would watch the news and shake his head at the senseless destruction caused by the machines produced by his Uncle's company and wonder how such violence could be perpetrated in the present, civilized age, insulated from his culpability by a brilliant ignorance.

Jenna's hunger for power was not a deep conviction. She alternated between humanitarian thoughts and mused about her own worth as a world leader. In truth, she simply wanted to be acknowledged and appreciated. For so much of her life, she felt invisible. She turned to the outrageous to gain recognition. Her hair, makeup, clothing, and stances were all designed to leave a memorable impression. However, when faced with the opportunity to assert her influence over this denizen of some other world, she fled.

Chris only lent her voice to their chants because of a desire to be close to Jeremy. She had a desperate crush on this unworthy man, did not realize her own value. When she witnessed the others flee the room, she was confused. She did not have an imagination that would allow her to glean the indications of the man's presence in the center of the room, nor was she curious enough to stay to learn the implications of their actions. She shrugged and walked up the stairs to follow the others.

Niles, shocked by their success, remained frozen. The hurried defection of over half of the group pleased him. "Fewer people to vie for supremacy," he reasoned, and wondered how to rid himself of the remaining man, Tom. He cleared his throat to create the most dramatic effect, wishing to set the ground rules, saying, "Ares, we summoned you and command you to do our bidding."

Ares turned a steely gaze on Niles, raising an ironic eyebrow. His face slowly broke into a broad, almost child-like smile that revealed protruding canines. "You? Command me?" He inquired, his voice a deep baritone like Japanese drums summoning troops to battle. He chuckled, a throaty rumble.

Niles gathered his wits and continued, sounding reasonable, "yes, as my captive, you will act according to my will." He nodded to reassure himself of this indisputable fact. A captured demon always had to fulfill the wishes of its master, the person who knew its name. Everything that he read expressed this truth.

Meanwhile, Tom inwardly cursed his equipment's brutal betrayal. He continued to quietly tinker with electronics, hoping for operation.

"Your captive, little man?" Ares tilted his head like a wolf contemplating its prey.

Niles adjusted his wire-rimmed glasses, becoming accustomed to this verbal chess match. "Clearly, I know your name. I have summoned you. You are held within this enchanted circle." He was feeling pleased with his logic.

Ares reared back his head and released a thunderous laugh, mirthless, self-aggrandized. "You believe that I am your captive?" He laughed again.

Niles reasoned, "Yes, I know that you are," pouring all of his conviction into his words. "You can't leave the circle."

"This circle?" Ares wondered, indicating the carefully yet inexpertly transcribed arcane symbols painted on the cement dormitory basement floor.

"Yes, sucker. That circle, and now you are going to do what I tell you," bullied Niles, emboldened in his imagined upper hand in the situation. Ares returned his gaze to Niles, lifted his leg, and stepped out of the circle with ease.

Niles turned pale, adjusted his glasses, and stepped back from the approaching Ares, gulping back an increasing panic. "Um, Ares, sir, no hard feelings, really. I just wanted to meet you, and honestly, it is such an honor," Niles simpered sycophantically, all boldness deflated. Ares continued his approach, unimpeded by any of the magical protections put in place by the college students. "You do not know my true name, mortal, but you will," Ares said. He reached out his left hand, holding his walking stick with his right, and grabbed Niles' neck. Niles' eyes bulged as in seconds, his larynx crushed. Ares carelessly discarded his still, staring body in a huddle in a dank basement corner, upsetting one of Tom's camcorders.

Tom remained frozen in another shadowy corner, seemingly unnoticed by the incarnation of the god of war. He watched as Ares ascended the basement stairs.

"Man, I'm missing history here." He forced himself to calm his shaking. Taking one of his hand-held devises, he followed at a careful distance. He skirted Niles' lifeless form. He witnessed Ares drop his walking stick, which transformed into a red Harley Davidson motorcycle. Ares then mounted, started the engine with a rumbling, leonine roar, and drove from the campus without a backward glance.

The campus ruled Niles' death a terrible accident, caused by a night of intoxication and a fall down the dangerous dormitory staircase. The dorm was better secured, the basement access locked. Rumors of occult symbols etched into the floor, of Niles being some sort of sacrifice, circulated and added to the character of the old campus.

Tom sold what he could salvage of the evening's footage to the New Science Channel. He was paid $12,000 for what would become a show hailed by conspiracy theorists and discounted by the majority of society. As he watched the changes in his already unstable world, he assumed the responsibility for his involvement. He hung himself in his dorm closet, the check from the New Science Channel uncashed and folded within his jeans' pocket.

All of the surviving group members found their sleep plagued by dreams of destruction after the night they summoned War. Their destinies altered, their souls disputed. They, as unwitting pawns, helped to break a seal, release a plague, bring about the end of days. Upon their consciences rested the buried knowledge that their actions began another great war, the last and worst. The gears of the war machine were of course already grinding, but without a focus.

They provided the leader who would guide the hawkish military leaders, filled their minds with battle lust and destruction. It was a war slow to consume, but ravenous, destroying entire populations. The contributions of ages of man lay waste, starting with the least civilized and progressing to societal giants.

Haiku 7

They had no notion

When they drew the pentagram

The Hell they'd release

Complacent Syrup

It bubbles there
beneath my skin
pulsing through my veins
pressing against my joints.

It cripples me,
locking out legs and hands
constricts my throat.

It scratches at my subconscious
invades my dreams
when I have a moment
to sleep,
an impetus percolating
like maniacal laughter.

It blinds with flashes,
sends chills racing along my spir.e,
deafens with its insistent roar.

I rock,
trying to sooth
what unsettles me,
but to no avail.

Should I slice through
the paper-thin skin
to free it,
or pray it settles
once again
into the complacent syrup
within me?

Brain Storm

Pounding in his aching head, the storm rises, reconfiguring thoughts. Like lightning, it sizzles, a blinding, maddening burst of clarity. The way became clear for just those seconds before the thunder of propriety and the law drowned the truth. After its echoes died away, he followed the charred course of the thoughts' passage, ignoring his burnt soles, his conflagrated soul, to reach the inevitable, murderous conclusion.

Sun and Sand

Timmy waved to the folks in the retreating brown station wagon, running down the suburban sidewalk to see his friends for as long as possible. His best friends, the Vandelier twins, laughed and waved with enthusiasm until the car rounded the bend and rolled out of sight. Timmy stopped and stood rooted like the tree beside him, an elm shading its namesake street.

The Vandelier family would return in two weeks from their trip to the beach.

Two weeks. An eternity!

Since Timmy's family hadn't the money for a summer vacation, they resolved to make the best of things at home. Berry picking in the local woods, chasing black and garter snakes through the high grass in the meadow, feeding ducks at the pond occupied his time. Mom sent him outside every chance she got. *She just wants to get rid of me so she can play with the baby.*

Her latest ploy involved his old sand box. "Pretend it is the beach. You can make sand castles."

"Mom, I'm not two, you know." He stomped. "This sucks. Why can't we go on a real vacation, too?"

Mom bounced the fussing baby on her shoulder and pressed her lips together in a tight line. Her slow blink indicated annoyance.

He felt heat rise in his cheeks. "Fine, fine, but this is the lamest summer break ever."

"Language, young man, and you could appreciate that you are out of school."

That's Mom for ya. Always saying stuff like that.

He threw the lid from the sandbox like a discus in an ancient Olympic Game. Mom sighed loud enough for him to hear, then took sobbing Sally into the house.

Buckets, shovels, and sieves waited his handiwork. Timmy sat on the edge, and ran his hand through the fine, warm grains. Pieces reflected the sunlight, transforming the homely bits into gold. He dug in deeper, feeling the sand massage up to his elbows. He closed his eyes and imagined the beach where crabs played in the surf at night. Waves polished sea glass and threw shells ashore. Pirates hid treasures and widows mourned their seamen on such land.

He felt something solid and long, a tree branch or something. He pulled. The sand poured off, a hissing spray as he pulled the object from his sandbox. As the last grains settled, Timmy tried to make sense of what he held. It looked and felt like a bone.

Why would a bone be in my sandbox?

He ran to the house. "Mom, look what I found! Mom? Mom!"

Mom met him at the door, a slender finger before her lips. "Shh, I just got your sister to sleep."

"But Mom, I found this in the sandbox."

She stared, her brow creased in consideration. "Did you get that from the Halloween decorations?"

"No, I told you, from the sandbox."

"That makes no sense. I just had your father fill that sand box."

He shrugged.

"Well, we'll ask your Dad when he gets home from work. In the meanwhile, go play."

Timmy took the bone and returned to the plastic turtle. *Wonder if there's any more in there?* He reached in, his arm slipping through the grains way past his elbow. Groping through, his arm sunk deeper. *But the box is only about ten inches deep. Is there a hole in the bottom?*

He felt another stiff form and grabbed. Another bone, this one with finger bones attached with some kind of rubbery stuff. He set it aside and dove in with both hands, leaning over the sun-warmed plastic. There was another, and another, and another. The pile of bones lay in a heap, a disassembled skeleton missing only the head.

Wonder if the pieces are all there, except for the head of course?

The boy pieced it together like in the forensics shows on his father's favorite night time television show, *The Dead Can Talk.*

You just need to listen.

But where is the head?

Can something talk if it doesn't have a head?

He sifted through the sand, searching for the skeleton's head, until the heels of his hands began to chaff. No luck. He tapped his knee with an agitated finger.

He addressed the bones displayed beside him. "I'll empty it of sand, real slowly. Then, I won't miss the head."

With careful scoops, he strained the sand through the sieve, each plastic shovelful scrutinized. When the box lay empty, the sand in anthill-like mounds nearby, Timmy turned the turtle over. No holes. Nothing underneath. He scratched his head.

The sun bore down, making the sweat tickle as it dribbled over his skin.

"Better cover you up," he said to the headless puzzle. "Be right back."

He ran through the house to the linen closet. He moved the folded sheet sets, searching for a white top sheet. *In the shows, they always cover the bodies with a flat white blanket of some sort.*

"Timothy Andrew McCarthy, why on earth are you running through my house, and why are you making a mess of the linen closet?"

"Just getting something to cover up the skeleton guy, Mom."

"What skeleton guy?"

An exaggerated sigh ripped through him until he drooped. "The bone that I showed you? There were a whole bunch in the sand box. A whole skeleton. Well, almost. It is missing a head. I want to cover it up."

"You are not covering up your dirty, sand-covered Halloween decoration with my clean linens. No way, Jose!"

"Mom, they are not decorations. They are really real bones from a person."

She stared at her son with narrowed, disbelieving eyes. "Not my linens."

He pressed his lips together, his lower lip jutting. "Fine, Mom. Just fine."

They stared at each other, like gunfighters sizing up opponents. "Run along," she said.

He stomped to his room and slammed the door.

I can't just leave the body lying there like that. It's not decent.

The door creaked as he crept from his room and entered his father's den. *The drop cloth covering Dad's traveling display case will do.* Creak. *Why do all of the doors in our house make noise?*

He tip-toed to the covered case in the corner. He looked over his shoulders to ensure he was unwatched, then snatched the rough drop cloth. He balled it up under his t-shirt, looking like a youthful, boyish pregnant lady. He prepared to dash out the door when something white in the case caught his attention and arrested movement. His breath caught in his throat.

He leaned his forehead against the case, scrutinizing the contents.

An aged skull smiled from atop a big, red book, props for Dad's part-time magic show. *Wonder if that is the skeleton's missing head?*

A lock prevented further exploration. *Drat. I'll ask Dad about it later.*

Blue and red lights transformed the eggshell living room walls into a dance hall.

His voice wavered. "Mom?"

A heavy knock at front door made him jump.

"Mom?" he yelled louder.

Carrying the baby, she stopped, mouth agape. "What's going on?"

"I don't know, but there's someone at the door." He removed the drop cloth from under his shirt as she answered.

"May I help you?"

The baby sniveled.

"Do you live here, Ma'am?"

"Of course. What's going on?"

"Are you aware there is a skeleton in your yard?"

Her eyebrows flew toward her hairline. She spun to her son. "Tim?"

His heart beat in his temples. He twisted the scratchy drop cloth in his hand. "I told you, Mom."

She looked younger as her confusion grew. She swung back to the black-clad officers at the door, bouncing the baby faster in her nervousness. "But it's a Halloween decoration, isn't it?" She turned back to her son. "Isn't it?"

Timmy wanted to hug his mother, to take the pale, scared look from her. Instead, he shrugged. *I told you.*

"We believe the remains are human, ma'am."

Mom sat on the floor at the officers' feet, any remaining color draining from her. The baby cried.

The officers helped her to the couch.

"What do you know about the remains, ma'am?"

"Nothing. My son was playing in the sandbox." She looked wide-eyed, mouth wide in shock. "Timmy, please talk to these officers. Tell them about the skeleton."

The men loomed large like nightmarish shadows. He gulped. "I was playing in the sandbox. I found the bones in there but I couldn't find..." He stopped. *The skull!* He clutched the drop cloth to his chin, breathing like a fish out of water.

"You couldn't find what, son?" Timmy stood walleyed and mute.

The officer on the left knelt before Timmy. "It's okay to talk to us, Timmy. We're here to help."

"I don't know where the bones came from. They were in the box."

"Were they assembled?"

He felt the heat rising through his chest and climb to his hairline. "No. I put them together."

The other officer pointed to the drop cloth. "What you got there, son?"

"I was gonna cover 'em up, like on the tv show. You know, *The Dead Can Talk*. My – Dad – likes that show. We watch it together on Tuesday nights at 8:00."

The officers stared, waiting for more information. "I know that show, Timmy."

"Do you know where the head is, son?"

He couldn't breathe. His voice sounded small. "I don't know." He stared at the carpeting.

The men looked at each other.

Mom said, "What happens now?"

"We'll take the bones in for examination and try to identify the deceased. We'll want to talk with your husband. Have him stop by the station house as soon as possible." He turned to Timmy and leaned in. "Son, if you find any other bones, you call us, you understand? It is not a game."

His face burned as he nodded, afraid to look into their eyes. *We need to vacuum.*

They handed business cards to Mom. "Call us if anything

occurs to you."

As they prepared to leave, Timmy asked, "Can the dead talk? You know, without their heads?"

The officer who knelt before him earlier turned. "Sometimes, but it's easier to i.d. a body with a head. Dental records. So, if you know where that skull is, we sure could use it."

Timmy nodded. "I'll let you know if I find it. It's not in the sandbox, though."

The officer ruffled Timmy's hair. They left, their muffled walkie-talkies sounding further away as they oversaw the bones' collection.

Timmy watched them finish up and leave. They took the sand, the sandbox, and the bones. He then went to the study and replaced the drop cloth. He peeked under at the skull. "Talk to me, please?"

The skull said nothing, just smiled its secrets.

"Fine," he said to the bones. "I'll ask Dad when he gets home."

Haiku 8

Time and temperature

Guide feeble footsteps deeper

Eager for the grave

Surrogate Sacrifice

Moira's socks slid on the hardwood flooring as she rushed to answer the door. She gasped. On the porch stood the biggest wooden crate she'd ever seen, outside of old-time mummy movies. She peered around its shadow to wave goodbye to the delivery driver before he sped from the driveway. "Guess he's afraid I'd ask him to help get this inside."

With a push, she tested the weight of the delivery. Even putting her shoulder into it yielded a mere budge. She squinted to read the packing label. *Dr. John O'Reilly.* Dear old Dad. Autumn cold sept through her socks, and she shivered. "Well, then, big boy, I can't move you on my own. Need to call in reinforcements." She dialed her father.

Excitement punctuated his words. "I'll find a crowbar and be right over."

The car threw gravel as her father rushed up the drive. He leapt from the car holding a tool and ran to the porch. The headlights spotlighted the package, blinding Moira when she opened the front door. She leaned on the doorframe while he set to work. The wood groaned and cracked with his efforts, revealing fine straw within.

He flung packing material and reached in. "Moira, help me with this."

Moira slouched opposite him.

"Push on three. One, two, three."

The carving felt warm despite the chill air. Moira stepped back. A toothy-grinned demon glared over the edge of the crate with baleful glee. She shivered in its shadow. "What the heck's this, Dad?"

He straining to take in the massive structure. "Isn't it beautiful? It's on loan for the museum."

She stepped away, uncomfortable beneath the statue's scrutiny. "Why'd it get sent here, then?"

He ran his hands down the smooth muscles in the statue's crouched legs. "Must've been a mistake, but maybe one we can use to advantage. Help me get it inside."

She scowled. "Can't you do it yourself?"

"No. Help me."

Moira shied away from placing her hands on the massive buttocks when she pushed.

"In the corner of the living room'll be perfect. Between the bookshelf and the fireplace." He grunted with effort. It nestled in as though the space were designed for it. He sighed. "Perfect."

Shadows playing across the statue's demonic features lent an imagined animation. "Uh, Dad, you're not going to leave it here, are you?"

"For a while. Isn't it magnificent?"

"Not what I'd call it, actually," she mumbled.

"Ancients claimed this effigy saved struggling communities when offered proper sacrifices. Thought it'd be cool to give the old ways a go, see if we can resurrect our stumbling society."

"With sacrifices?"

"I've some calls to make."

"Wait, Dad, what kind of sacrifices?"

He backed from the figure as though reluctant to turn away. He reached and ruffled her hair. "You know, the usual. Blood of the firstborn." He laughed as he hurried to his den.

She crossed her arms over her chest and glowered. "Well, he's not spilling my blood. Already scares the crap out of me, creeping around my room at night. Thinks I don't see him, but I do." She slumped into an overstuffed seat. "Don't know what I'll do if he ever touches me. Can't sleep right anymore." Tears slid over her cheeks. She blew her nose, throwing the wadded tissue at the statue. "Here's my sacrifice. Now do something useful, will ya?" She rushed upstairs, threw herself on her bed, and nodded off.

A knock startled her. "Moira, I'm having a few colleagues over. Put together some canapés. Oh, and wear something nice. Thanks."

She punched her pillow. "Seriously? What now?" She donned a dress and made up a tray the way her mother had taught her before she died.

Dr. Rowan from the archaeology department swiped a snack as Moira set out the food. "You've grown into quite a young woman, Moira."

Moira forced a smile. Beneath the gaping grin of the sculpture, her father called for attention. "Thank you for coming. You know why we're here. Everyone have offerings? Good. Let's make our museum a success, shall we?" The group chuckled. "Let me introduce my beautiful daughter." Everyone turned toward Moira, many raising glasses as in a toast.

She felt a blush consume her and tugged at her collar, ducking her chin to disguise discomfort. Someone clapped Moira on her shoulder, pushing her toward her father's outstretched hand. He caught her wrist and tugged. His smile sent shivers up her spine. The room erupted in monotonous intonations from close-eyed scholars.

Moira yanked at his vice-like grip. "Hey! What're you doing?"

The guests' voices unified.

"Let me go, Dad. You're hurting me."

Everyone stared at the figure, Moira, and her father. He patted her trapped hand. "You know our organization has fallen on hard times. Our friends at The Ludworth Society sent this god. They assure us the old ways can restore our good standing. Worked for them." His voice cracked, and he withdrew something from his vest pocket. "For the good of all."

The group nodded, fever-brightness lighting their eyes.

"The first offering sets the tone for the ceremony." A knife glinted. He slid it across her wrist. Blood spurted, and Moira screamed. He pulled her into an awkward embrace. She screeched as he attacked again.

Grinding behind them, and the animated statue plucked the weapon before it drew more blood. A pandemonium of retreat ensued. The stone hand closed on her father's throat; his eyes bulged, and his face reddened as he gasped. Moira gripped her sliced wrist and backed away.

Dr. Rowan handed Moira a linen napkin without looking at her. "You said it yourself, Dr. O'Reilly. The first sacrifice sets the tone for the ceremony."

He pounded and kicked against the carved stone. He gasped, "Didn't finish sacrifice."

Dr. Rowan pointed to the statue clutching the tissue Moira had thrown. "Guess yours wasn't the first sacrifice." She turned Moira. "We'd better clean you up, Moira dear. I think your request's being granted."

Haiku 9

Within realms burst free

Filled with vibrance and color

Business suit confined

After Disaster

"You're playing a dangerous game," Paul said, dark eyes twinkling.

Birdie refused to allow Paul or his wicked grin to distract her. She squinted at the pieces, imagining the future based on her move. "Yeah, but if I lose, all it'll cost me is a kiss. You'll owe me dinner if – when – I win." She slid her bishop into place.

"Confidence. I like it." He moved his bishop.

She smiled, admiring his black emergency worker uniform and kind, pale face. "Do you play chess with all your rescues?" She engaged her queen.

"Just the most interesting." He sidled his knight, an unanticipated move that decimated her strategy. Realizing her mistake, she scrambled to correct. Smoke from the nearby wreckage clouded her vision.

Paul's crew chief stopped, sighing. "Really, son, again? Chess?"

Paul shrugged. "Passing time until we can get everyone where they're going. Might as well enjoy ourselves?" He winked at Birdie whose face grew hot.

She interposed her castle.

He took it. "Check. Your move."

Her heart raced. Checkmate loomed.

She sat back, giggled, and twirled a strand of hair to distract him. "You know, if we were on a beach, this would be like that Ingmar Berman movie I studied in film history."

He cocked his head, amused. "How astute. You're really clever." He waved his hand over the board. "Your move."

She swallowed. "I'm not going to survive this, am I?"

Sadness clouded his face. He tapped a pawn, considering. "Where would you have liked to eat, if you won?"

She looked at her bandaged wounds. Blood seeped in gory patterns, runes to be interpreted by another generation. "I suppose anywhere would do."

He leaned across the board. "You're in luck. You'll never be hungry." Paul took her queen. "Checkmate."

Haiku - 0

Sleep weighs heavily

Nightmare sits upon the chest

Crushed hope-filled dreaming

Bad News

The telephone screamed for attention. Heidi lunged for the receiver. Her baby just fell asleep, and she wanted to keep him that way.

"Hello, Heidi? You're not going to believe this, but Malcolm Westran is dead. I just read about it in the paper."

"Holly? Oh my gosh! How did he die?"

"He lost control of his bike while travelling on the Turnpike."

"I didn't know he had a bike. I've not seen him in years, though. Crap. I can't believe he's dead! He's, what, thirty-three?"

"Yeah, we graduated with him. Know what's worse? His daughter and girlfriend were in their car behind him when it happened."

Heidi slumped into a kitchen chair. "That's awful. How old's his kid?"

The sound of paper rustling, preceded Holly's response. "Says she's twelve."

"Wait, twelve? That means I should know the kid. I didn't know he had a kid, especially not a twelve-year-old. Ryan and I still hung out with him when we were in our early twenties, before he got heavy into drugs. He never said a word about a kid."

"Dunno. But it says that Malcolm Westran of Bessemer died yesterday."

"Bessemer is small, that's for sure. Gotta be him. Man, that sucks."

"Gotta go make calls. See you at lunch Thursday?"

"Looking forward to it." Heidi shook her head and stared at the receiver. She texted her husband.

Do you remember Malcolm Westran? You aren't gonna believe this. He's dead. Died on the Turnpike yesterday.

She started a pot of coffee, and when ready, she poured a cup and drank it black. The bitter flavor suited her mood.

When they were friends, Malcolm was fun. His silly sense of humor kept them in stitches. She recalled hanging at the beach with a group of friends. Malcolm set up a bonfire and told scary stories in the evening. He hosted trampoline and pool parties in his back yard, and if a party took place, he provided comic relief.

When he started taking heavy drugs, their friendships fell apart.

"I never told him he should stop. I never told him that was why we stopped being his friend," she said out loud, hunched over the coffee mug.

A jingle announced a text message.

You gotta be kidding me! Did you tell Jeevies? Ray-Ray?

I guess I will. Should we go to the funeral?

Heck yes. Poor guy.

Heidi felt tears prickle at her eyes.

'Too young to die. Damn.'

She texted the sad news to her friends.

An answering text made her cry.

Surprised he made it this long. Poor junkie.

She swiped her eyes, sniffing as she wiped down the kitchen, keeping busy. The phone rang. She ran to answer.

"Hello?"

"Hi! Heidi?"

She would not have recognized the voice if he weren't fresh in her mind. She gripped the counter. "Malcolm? Holy crap! I heard that you died."

"Yeah, that's why I'm calling. Some other poor dude in Bessemer with my name, I guess. I'm still alive."

"Oh, thank God! Shoot, I wonder what happened?"

"Don't know. Don't have a bike. Not dead. Call off the troops, will yah?"

"Of course, of course! Oh my gosh, I am so glad that you are okay! You don't have a kid, do you?"

"Nope."

"Do you still live in Bessemer?"

"Yep, same house and everything. Taking care of my

mom."

'This is a rare opportunity,' Heidi thought, 'to fix a mistake of the past.'

"Listen, I don't mean to be rude or invasive, but are you still taking drugs?"

A pause, then he cleared his throat.

"It's none of my business, but that was why we drifted apart. You are a great guy. Please don't waste your life."

"Yeah, thanks. Take care."

She hung up and texted their friends the good news.

Haiku 11

Come wayward traveller

Enjoy a luxury stay

With the ages' dead

Black Jack

(Dedicated to the Daytime Writers, Springdale, PA)

Police men's voices sounded muffled, as though coming through the walkie- talkies at their utility belted waists instead of their mouths. "Ma'am, we're going to file this report at the station. If anything else occurs to you, you have our cards." They touched their hats like cowboys as they left.

McKenzie did not look up as she mechanically thanked the two young, uniformed men. "I'd show you photographs of my furnishings if they hadn't taken my photo albums, too," she'd explained to them. She looked at the built-in book shelf beside the red brick fireplace, and tears prickled at her eyes for the first time since she returned from their vacation.

Make-a-Wish had granted a trip to Walt Disney World in sunny Florida to her daughter, 13 year old Amanda. It was the kindest experience they had ever experienced, with no worries to trouble sleep and less pain since Amanda's last surgery. They came home to a house that was clean. They usually had a tidy house, but this was scrubbed top to bottom. No cob webs. No dust. No personal effects either. The windows curtains and blinds remained intact and closed, but everything else, from clothing to the dressers that held them, silly mementos magnetted to the refrigerator and the fridge itself, even the toiletries and toilet paper in the bath, gone. No welcome mat to greet them at their front door, nor a boot tray to host their muddy shoes when they entered the Victorian charmer in the quiet Verona neighborhood.

The only thing remaining was a single playing card, face up, dead center in the living room. McKenzie stared at the one-eyed Jack, her emotion hidden, when she answered the questions from the police in their black uniforms. She lied when they asked if the card held any special meaning to her, denied the truth that he had found them after so many years of careful hiding. He'd wanted her to know who now possessed her possessions, know that he would be coming for them.

She locked and dead bolted the heavy front door. No signs of forcible entry.

Her footfalls echoed through the hollowed-out room, a sound that resonated within her hollowed-out self. She turned a false smile to her daughter standing in the living room where their couch would have been, her Disney princess shirt brilliantly pink. McKenzie had two hundred dollars left from the trip, and not much in her bank accounts, but it would have to do.

"We are going on a new adventure, Amanda," McKenzie exclaimed, "Since we are already packed, we are ready to go. Where would you like to live, my love, and what name do you think is the prettiest?"

Amanda furrowed her brow. She was a trusting and caring child, her thirteen years sheltered and youthful. "Jasmine, momma, like on this shirt." She pointed to the dark-haired beauty, and McKenzie smiled. "I like that name, too, Jasmine. What about me, though?" Amanda liked this game, so she clapped. "Princess names are fun! What about Ariel?"

"How about Jane, like in Tarzan?"

"Oh, I like Jane, and you look pretty in yellow!"

"Great! We are Jasmine and Jane Darling, okay?"

"I love our names!" The child shuffled around the house. "But where's our stuff?"

She hugged her girl. "Stuff doesn't matter. We have each other. Where should we live?"

"Disney!"

"I don't think we can live there, silly!"

"Florida, then?"

She considered her finances. "How about someplace a little closer, but still warm?"

She did not care where they lived. Her one criterion was it needed to be someplace new to hide the two of them from an abuser, a place to shelter them from a one-eyed, black-hearted Jack to whom one was married and the other never called Daddy.

Haiku 12

Creeks and groaning joints

Rusting promise decaying

Abandoned childhood

Blood Bond

Bright as a blood bond, it flashed into Linda's periphery, a cardinal hopping in the snow-covered holly outside her window. Its incongruity caught her attention, and it intrigued. She struggled with bedding caught in the rough casts on her left arm and her right leg to slide the window open. A blast of cold assaulted, and she shivered.

The bird paused to cock its head before hopping to another branch, dislodging a sprinkle of dislodged snow.

Linda's tears welled but did not fall. She clutched the snowy window ledge to steady herself as a wave of nausea threatened to overtake her. "What? What do you want?"

The bird left footprints as it went about its business, but they spelled out no message.

Linda scooped a handful of snow with her right hand, rolled it on the ledge until it compressed into a loose ball. "Fine. Leave me alone then." It turned away, and she threw her snowball at the bird. It fluttered off with a quiet rush of red through the stark landscape. She pulled the window shut and collapsed into her pillows. She ignored her throbbing body aches and the hot tears that cooled on her cheeks.

Her little brother Sigurd lingered in her door way

clutching his teddy bear, unspoken words heavy on his lips. She barked, "What do you want?" He fled to the shadows, away from her anger and grief. Guilt from mistreating him added another weight to her accumulated burden, and she sobbed, harsh, racking moans pulled from deep in her soul. She racked her fingernails into her flesh until angry tracks marked their progress.

Her mother rushed into the room to wrap her in a hug. "Honey, please. This is not good for you."

Linda melted into her comfort for a moment, but in a blinding rush pushed her away. She deserved no comfort. "Leave me alone!"

Her mother held on, stroking her hair like she did during Linda's childhood. "Sh, honey. It's okay."

Linda shoved her mother. "No, nothing's okay, Mother! Nothing will be ever again!" She shook with repressed rage. "Get out."

Her mother handed her a medicine cup and glass of water.

"I don't want any more pills."

"Can't let the pain get ahead of you. Now take it."

Her mother would not leave unless she took the medicine. Linda trembled as she swallowed the pill and chased it with water. It stumbled around the area of her healing trach. A permanent lump in her upper throat swelled with outrage.

Her mother rested a gentle hand on her forehead, smoothing hair from her face. "That will help soon."

As her mother left, Linda realized it wouldn't. No medicine would help. Not soon or ever. She closed her eyes, but visions of the crash assailed her. She jerked from the nightmare and cried in silence.

Despite her determination to ignore the smell of holiday cooking, Linda's traitorous stomach rumbled with anticipation. Turkey and stuffing, pies and breads. Sigurd sung a holiday song in the kitchen as he fetched spices for mom. "Is this ginger?" he asked, and mom laughed. "No, silly, that's garlic. It would not taste good in our sweet potatoes." A knock at the front door interrupted their giggles. Linda pulled the duvet over her head to block out the cheerful sounds of normality. Didn't they know normal was a torturous Hell for her now?

A gentle pressure and the smell of chopped onions announced her mom's presence "Honey, Mrs. Burns is here to see you."

Linda pushed the duvet from her face, scowling. "I don't want to see anyone, Mom."

Her mother set a hand on Linda's cheek. "She'll only be a moment." She whispered, "Please, honey, everyone is mourning. Of course, Karen's mother is in pain, but she needs to see you."

Fear joined the tangled knot of guilt settled within her, frigid as ice. Her lips trembled, but she saw determination in her mother's eyes. "Fine. But give me my brush."

Her mother pinched her lips over a retort, but fetched the tool. "Do you want me to braid your hair?"

Linda trembled. She masked fear with an outburst. "Oh my gosh, mother! I'm not a child. I don't need you to braid my hair."

Her mother nodded and left her to rip tangles from unruly hair. She poured self-loathing into her merciless pursuit of knots, tearing clumps. Not a child, no. She would graduate from high school soon. State University accepted her for the upcoming year. She worked to pay for her insurance and earned her driver's license this autumn, or had before the accident. Tears made silent progress over burning cheeks.

Karen Burns' mother deserved to come, to unload hatred on her daughter's killer. Linda searched for an escape. Snow swirled outside, and the cardinal returned to regard her with eyes like shining seeds. There was no running from what she'd done. Time to own up. Besides, Mrs. Burns could not detest her more than she detested herself. She steeled herself for the deserved onslaught.

Her mother and Mrs. Burns entered while Linda

scrubbed tears from her face. Dressed in black, Mrs. Burns looked older than when last Linda saw her, the day she and Karen left for a party. Linda shuddered at the memory of her best friend's promise to "be careful."

Mrs. Burns cleared her throat. "How are you feeling?"

Linda shrugged, unwilling to trust her voice.

"I won't keep you, dear. I know you're in pain." Mrs. Burns blinked back tears. Linda responded in kind. "But I needed to drop this off for you." She held out a present wrapped in prismatic silver. "It's from Karen." Her voice broke, and she coughed into her shoulder. "She was working on it before…" Her words hung like an ominous storm cloud.

Before Karen died. Because of Linda. Linda who was not a child, but could drive to parties on her own.

The package rested on her lap atop the chaffing, thigh-high cast. As a child, she'd broken her wrist while bike riding with Karen. She'd misjudged a turn. Karen had decorated the resulting cast with colorful illustrations reminiscent of the matching tattoos they later planned for when they turned eighteen. Linda's current casts remained barren.

"Go on, honey," her mother encouraged. "Open it."

She slid a finger beneath the wrapping, taking care not to rip the paper. Had Karen taped it? From the shape and feel of the package, she guessed the contents. One of Karen's fanciful pieces of art.

On the canvas, two birds huddled beneath a canopy of cherry blossoms, their heads together as though conspiring. Linda ran her finger along the evident brush strokes, admiring her friend's talent. Paint transformed into an idyllic scene what once was blank. She whispered, "Beautiful."

Transfixed by the gift, Linda startled when Mrs. Burns touched her shoulder. "May I see it, please?"

Linda turned the canvas. Tears clouded her vision as she watched Mrs. Burns struggle to maintain composure. She gasped, "I've heard cardinals bring messages from departed loved ones." She touched a trembling finger to the birds. Shadows darkened around her furrowed brow, and her lip trembled. "She made something for me, too. See?" Mrs. Burns extended a ceramic pendant depicting a lily. "Lovely, isn't it?"

Linda nodded. She remembered Karen baking it in the kiln during their art class. "Mom'll love this. It's her favorite flower," she'd said.

"Mrs. Burns," Linda's voice sounded small. "I'm so sorry."

Mrs. Burns rested a hand atop Linda's casted arm. "I know you are." Tears transformed her makeup into caricatures of French clowns. "Get better." Her footfalls clomped a sad retreat, and Linda's mother saw Mrs. Burns to the door.

Sigurd crept up to Linda's bed and pointed. "That's the same kind of birdie." The cardinal on her window sill tilted its head as though in salute before flying into the greying night.

Haiku 13

Stitched smiles, simpered sighs

She clings to an illusion

Death imitates life

Devil's in the Details

Collin found my sanctuary in a dusty steamer trunk in his Great-Aunt Kelly's attic. He blew across my book's* cover, and his breath sent a thrill through me. I beckoned, a silent entreaty, hoping the chipped gilding might intrigue. He ran a finger along leather supple as a lover's hand, and he felt my shivered anticipation.

The spine creaked when opened, but I am over 1300 years old. Such an advanced age does present certain challenges. With a puff, I sent forth perfume redolent with ink and vanillin, resin and terpene. Calligraphed and illuminated, each page drew him closer to the inevitable. I collected myself in the corners of pages, peeked from behind illustrations, and hid between words.

Daylight wasted, yet he could not abandon his find. He searched for me without realization, abandoned reason to answer a primal pulse. As though he'd dreamed me into life, though my existence outstripped his ancestry. I coalesced from inferences and allusions. He muttered an invocation without realizing his lips moved. Each syllable fortified me.

I strengthened until at last I strode from my hiding place.

His eyes bulged like a comic imitation of a frog when I coiled my intentions around his neck. He gasped a protest I ignored.

I absorbed his essence, pulled his pigments into a margin where I trapped him, a caricature of himself, an amphibian caught within strangling vines.

The book in question is a unique volume titled "The Codex of St. Isidore" from 666 AD. To survive the Viking conquests, monks secreted the volume to Durham and later Bath, thereby narrowly escaping destruction. It reappeared in London in 1558 AD. The British Library digitized the 333 vellum sheets, and guests can view the complete volume online.

Haiku 14

Time-thief of beauty

Decay eroded dreams

Return to stardust

Grimoire

With satisfaction, Jenna closed the tome, a resounding thud marking the conclusion of years of research. She felt liberated, but as with most commitments, the end was bittersweet. She could now present her findings, speak with additional authority, yet something pulled at the recesses of her imagining, fluttering as insubstantially as a sigh.

Completing this project meant tenure at the university and a coveted seat among her fellows. Financial freedom and intellectual independence, an upgraded office, and paid research assistants were also longed-for perks, ending years of struggle. Her compiled work would be printed and bound, revered for generations, a defining piece on a controversial subject.

For years, her students looked askance and the staff, in hushed voices, made light of Jenna's work. However, she learned to comprehend cuneiform and hieroglyphics. She was renowned for her translations from ancient Greek and Aramaic. Archaeological digs in Uruk, Egypt, and the Holy Lands benefitted from her assistance, and she came away from the experiences with additions to her life's work, her personal Grimoire.

Jenna rolled her head in a circle, hoping to ease some of the tension built up in her neck and shoulders. Hunching over books and pouring through their archaic knowledge exacted a price in muscle soreness and impacted vision. Jenna looked down at the heavy wood library table, bemused by the completion of the task, when her attention was drawn to the back of her own right hand.

There, among the veins, written in black ink on her sun-deprived skin, was a message. The lettering was tiny but unmistakably Jenna's own handwriting. She looked closer, wondering why she could not remember writing on herself. She squinted, then retrieved a magnifying glass to peer closer and piece together the words.

"Each heartbeat draws you closer, each breath pushes away. Pursue the working wisdom that precedes the end of days. For the passing of time is marked in simple, gentle acts. Consider well your eternal soul before displaying facts."

She straightened, gently setting aside the magnifying glass. Lost in thought, she rubbed her left hand over the printing. "Consider well your eternal soul…" During the twenty years spent immersed in occult texts, Jenna questioned the theology in which she was raised. She redefined her beliefs with exposure to mysteries and alternative thinking, abandoned some core aspects while embracing others. Looking at a glowing screen on which she wrote, she considered her soul, her youthful hopes, and her adult dreams.

End of days, the time of sorting, goats and sheep and virgin rewards. Jenna did not necessarily believe in magic, did not practice any of what she learned, but she did compile a definitive look into the systems of those who did. This overview could guide a reader from a heavenly path. Then again, she reasoned, thinking of her vast investment into the research, the information is available, just not as readily as presented in her work.

She pushed her chair back from the desk and stretched her arms skyward. "With great power comes great responsibility," Uncle Ben told Peter Parker as he donned the mask of Spiderman.

She felt her own irregular heartbeat, her finger poised over the delete button on her tablet.

Haiku 15

Headache slashes through

Serial slaughter of thought

Incomprehension

Homecoming

Henry Dashell tensed, alert and confused, when the kitchen door swung open. Only he and close family used that entrance.

"Stay here," he whispered to his girlfriend Layla. He handed his wine goblet to her and tip toed to the kitchen, grabbing a Louisville Slugger on the way for protection.

He peeked around the corner. Overhead florescent lighting cast a bluish look on the white tile. Muddy footprints led to the powder room beside the pantry. A cloying smell akin to rotting floral arrangements sitting in stagnant water assaulted. He wiped a hand across his nose and fought back a gag. With steady steps, he crept to place his ear to the white-washed door.

Within, a woman hummed as she splashed in the water. He stumbled back, nearly dropping the bat. His mouth opened in a caricature of shock. The cooktop island arrested his progress, pressing into the small of his back.

The door creaked like old bones on a cold day, opening with painful slowness. He choked as a stench proceeded a naked foot not entirely rid of Georgia clay. The lace hem of a Sunday dress, a blue sash, her favorite strappy shoes.

He blinked back disbelief, finding it difficult to breathe from fear and the stench. The ever-present gold-and-diamond locket still shone around her throat, but her hair fell in a tangled mess over her shoulders. She wiped her face with a washcloth, hiding her features. She continued to hum the lullaby they had used to calm their children.

She had always prided herself on her manicure. Now, the nails split into their quick, dirt caked into the beds and fingerprints, a bit of pink polish clinging like broken bits of glass along a highway. The skin peeled back from her fingers, revealing gravel-laced flesh and bits of bone.

She lowered the cloth, confirming his suspicion. He staggered. Josephine, his deceased wife, arrived home.

She smiled when she spotted him. "Hello darling." Her voice rattled from within her chest like a panther's purr. She tossed the filthy cloth to the counter behind her.

"I had the worst dream. A man gave me the worst facial and makeup job, then put me in a tanning bed and forgot me. Then, I found myself trapped in the dark." A glaze floated across her eyes, obscuring her irises and pupils like cataracts. "You wouldn't believe how hard it was to find my way out so that I could come home."

With a shudder, he considered her hands.

"Don't you want to kiss me?"

He felt his freshly-consumed wine revolting within him.

He slid along the island countertop, backing away from her.

"Joey," tears sprung to his eyes. "You aren't supposed to be here."

"Why not? This is my home."

A woman's voice behind made him jump. "Because, Josephine, you're dead."

Nobody moved. Henry feared glancing at Layla, feared turning away from Josephine whose face's blue tones darkened.

Josephine pinched her lips and narrowed her diseased eyes. "Why Layla Cornwall, as I live and breathe."

"Not any more, Josephine."

Josephine rounded on Henry, the stench of the grave coating his face as she hissed, "Have you taken up with the likes of Layla Cornwall?"

Henry gulped, bending back across the counter to escape.

Josephine asked, "But where are my children?"

Henry's throat whistled like a gentle wind through autumn leaves, an unintelligible hiss.

Layla drawled, "They're safe and asleep."

Josephine lurched toward Layla, leaning to look into her eyes. Layla stood her ground.

She wheeled on Henry, skeletal arm pointing to Layla. "Did you replace me with this baggage?"

Henry looked at the dark, congealed blood on her toes. He

whispered, "Joey, you're dead."

Yellow oozed from Josephine's tear ducts, making slow progress to her jaw. "That's it, then? You don't need me? The kids don't need me?"

Layla rested a hand on Josephine's thin shoulder. "Bless your confused soul, of course they need you. They'll always love you. They'll carry you in their hearts for the rest of their lives. But they're alive, and you're not."

"Fine." Josephine said and dropped to the floor, inanimate, dead again.

Haiku 16

Amassed sins broke souls

Beautific smile upon lips

Angel falls from grace

Influential Spirit

Spirits influence people.

Juan learned the truth one night after a hard day of work at the gasket factory. He and some co-workers visited the local bar. They waited for a table to open. All the space jockeys hogged the seats at the bar, laughing with raucous abandon while they bragged of their latest cargo haul through the outlining galaxies.

When a group of Maribars from the Andromeda Galaxy left, Juan and his friends rushed like a football line to secure their table. They bussed it themselves and ordered round after round of drinks.

Before long, Juan, drunk on spirits, proposed creating an invention. The others laughed, thumped him on the back, and bought him a last beer for the road. "Always the same thing. Juan gets drunk and crazy-talks about his time machine."

"It's not crazy-talk, I tell you! All I have to do is figure out a way to make the structure strong enough to withstand the pull. It's like passing through a worm hole, you know, or a black hole."

They took their leave, and Juan carried his stein of beer for the walk home. As he mounted the stairwell for the retro brownstone, he noticed a jockey leaning against the doorframe. The attention the stranger directed made Juan feel uncomfortable. He forced his non-compliant legs to steady and stood as straight as the dizzying world allowed. The plan – to walk passed without a further glance at the stranger – failed when Juan stumbled on the top step and fell head-long into the stranger. Or rather the wall behind the stranger. Juan fell through the stranger as though he were made of no more than frozen mist.

He pushed back, rubbing his throbbing head, thinking, *How drunk am I?*

The stranger crossed his arms over his expensive leather vest, shook his head, and tutted his tongue. "That was unpleasant, mate. Let's not do that again, alright?"

"How'd you do that? Disappear like that?" Juan reached toward the stranger.

The stranger stepped away from Juan's reach. "That'll be enough of that tonight, Juan. We've work to do."

"Work? What kind of work?" He'd lust left eight and a half hours filled with gaskets. Work didn't sound like any fun. "Hold on a second! How'd you know my name?"

"Great, so you don't remember me? Again? Really, Juan, this grows tiresome. Let's get some coffee into you and work on that time machine."

Juan startled, tripping over his own feet and nearly falling back down the stairs before righting himself by slamming the beer around the door jam. He squinted at the stranger, forcing coherent thought through his befuddled brain.

"How'd you know about the time machine?"

The stranger ignored his question and proceeded Juan up the stairs to his second-floor apartment.

"You need to use steel reinforced with enamel. It will do the trick."

"Like, um, a bathtub? The old fashioned kind?"

"Isn't that why you rented this dump? For the retro styling of the place? Now get to work."

The next morning, dusty sunlight streamed through the window unimpeded, because the curtain rod lay unburdened on the floor. Juan groaned. The beams exacerbated his hangover headache. On the toilet seat sat his half-consumed beer.

"Hair of the dog," he said, taking a swig. Juan stepped out of the bathtub time machine, grateful for the beer, unaware of his accomplishment.

From the corner of the room, the invisible spirit of the space jockey sighed.

"He's not drunk enough to see me now, and the moron's forgotten again." He punched at the wall with all his aggression. The resulting gentle knock caused Juan's head to pound anew. The spirit shook its head. "Guess I'll try again next week."

Jurogumo

He tipped his glass to her, and she coyly lowered her almond eyes, blushing as she accepted the chocolate martini. He confidently moved to the bar stool beside her. Her exotic beauty enticed many glances, so he wanted to establish possession with body language and proximity.

She was slight built, doll like. He admired the way the clothes clung to her athletic curves as she reminisced about Japan. A song played, causing a moue on her small red lips.

"Are the singers in pain or angry?" She wondered aloud.

"Both, maybe. I don't know." He smiled slyly, "but we could go someplace with music that you might like better."

He congratulated himself when she offered to play for him on her lute. Her apartment was not far. Though he had no idea what a lute was, this privacy was better then he'd hoped. He watched her tight behind sway enticingly as she proceeded, anticipating the feel of her tiny waist.

He never asked her name. She offered it anyway, an enticement and a warning. "Jurogumo." He did not speak Japanese, and she did not translate, just smiled sweetly. Her own anticipation, that of the "whore spider," was eating her willing fly.

Laundry Day

Under normal circumstances, I wouldn't be caught dead in a place like this. Since my husband lost his job, though, we don't have enough money to repair our washing machine. Five children and we two adults generate a lot of laundry.

I struggled with the plastic baskets, the handles biting into my fingers and palms. Ice made walking precarious. I bumped the frozen door with my behind to gain admittance to the Brite and Shiny Laundry Facility. The quarters in my wristlet clinked.

The January sun shone weak and ineffectual. The frigid temperature allowed frost to form thick on both sides of the windows. The effect reminded me of our bathroom window, translucent enough to admit light, yet as obscuring and stained glass. I felt grateful for the obstructed view.

Though a place to clean garments, the Brite and Shiny was filthy. No attendant oversaw the machines.

A sign written with black marker on a piece of paper read, "Trouble? Call 1-444-678-5978."

Lint, thick as rodent fur, collected in corners and under folding counters. The trash bins overflowed with empty soap containers and discarded junk. The soda machine was broken.

No big loss, though. I did not have extra change. A crackling speaker played tunes from my high school years, classics or oldies depending on the station.

Inside of the gloomy room, the air smelled of detergent and fabric softening sheets. The humidity within felt nice compared to the negative twenty wind-chill factor that awaited outside.

I loaded a bay of large washers, pouring coins into the slots. A book, the latest best-selling horror work, kept me company during the process.

A man struggled with a plastic tub. I held the door to help, grateful for anonymity. He smiled in thanks. I nodded and returned to my position. We were the only people present.

A shrieking bell announced the wash cycle's conclusion. I pulled the damp, wadded loads into a silver wheeled cart to transport them to the opposite wall with the dryers. My daughter's favorite jumper, blue with a squirrel capering across, fell. I contemplated re-washing it, but I decided against it. I transferred clothes, dryer sheets atop, inserted coins and pressed start. I looked for my book but could not find it.

"Where you from?" the man leaned against the washing machine. I guessed his age as early thirties, clean-shaven and reasonably good looking.

"Local," I said, checking the cart for my reading material.

"Is that your Cadillac out there?"

Of course it is, I thought. No one else graced the place. I nodded at him, tapping my manicured fingernails on the Formica folding counter. My engagement ring flashed above the wedding band in the flickering florescent lighting. *Where could that book be?*

"Hotel California" struggled through the popping speakers. "You can check out any time you like, but you can never leave."

I bent down to check under the counter.

I never saw the blow, but I felt my skull crush in. My consciousness floated from my pain-racked body. I drifted to the ceiling, near the speaker and watched as he used a heavy wooden hanger to smear my brain across the unmopped floor. The dryers stopped. He stepped over me to my purse. He grabbed my little money and credit cards, then he dumped the contents. My kids' pictures smiled from the mess. A pouch of makeup and medical cards, two plastic army men, my cellular phone, and a satchel with pads he ignored, but my car keys he claimed.

I watched him leave, a strange detachment fogging my reactions until I realized that as a ghost, I would be caught dead here.

Little Washerwoman

Tomas woke from a pleasant dream to an unpleasant reality. The room felt uncomfortable and cold, so cold he saw his breath curling from between his lips. He must have slept wrong on his left arm and shoulder. He felt stiff and sore, and deep breaths hurt.

Why am I up at 3:30 in the bloody morning? He wondered.

He froze. *Was that crying?*

He struggled with the sweat-covered sheets.

Sweat on a cold night? Why is it so cold?

His bare feet touched the tiled floor. His wife insisted the stone reminded her of their homeland. Of Scotland. He wanted soft, plush carpet. He turned to his wife, sleeping in the bed. The auburn clung to her hair, defiant of the encroaching gray, as though defining her unique, obstinate personality. He reached a trembling hand to touch the soft curls flowing like lava across her pillow. The movement sent a sharp pain up his arm and through his left side.

He decided to walk. He grabbed his tartan-inspired robe and squirrel-embroidered slippers and made his way to the thermometer in the living room. The temperature registered at the typical 70 degrees. He turned it up to 74 to hear the furnace kick on and be certain that it worked. It roared into life, rustling papers on a book shelf.

The crying caught his attention again. A child or a woman wailed outside. He opened the oaken front door, hoping to see high winds wailing, but outside sat still and calm. The landscaping looked like a fairyland by moonlight. Though late, fireflies flashed a path toward the stream. He smiled, recalling boyhood hunts for the shining creatures with his older brothers and sister.

Missing them made his chest feel tight.

The crying came from near the stream. He made his way across the lawn, listening to the night music of frogs and crickets, rustling undefined in the holly and the quiet *whoosh* of bats overhead.

He saw a woman at the bank, her long, red curls dipping into the stream. A fog crept from the ground, engulfing his feet and encircling her. She knelt by the stream, washing a piece of linen, wailing like a distant storm. Despite rubbing it against the rocks, her efforts did nothing to remove the stain on the cloth.

"Lass, are ye alright? Please don't be cryin'."

She gazed into his eyes, and he recognized her, the little washer woman, the banshee. His heart clenched, seized. He clutched at the pain, but he knew his time on this earth ended.

Coffee and Scones

The onus of preparing the snacks for The Book Club always fell on Belinda. The other members spent their time complaining about health concerns and lifetime ills. As the youngest affiliate, 59-year-old Belinda's grievances found little sympathy among her fellows.

Belinda mixed the dry ingredients and added the moist. She crafted two batches of scones, one traditional and the other with chocolate chips, both boasting her secret ingredient. The smells of browning quick-bread made her stomach grumble. "Not yet," she thought, clutching her stomach. "For the book club gals."

She ground the beans and percolated coffee. She poured French roast into a travel carafe, Decaf into a second, and pumpkin spice in a third. She held her breath as she filled plastic baggies labeled 'sweetener.' Plastic spoons and knives, insulated cups, butter packets, and paper plates slid beside the warm food. As a special treat, she included a bouquet of roses, one for each of the participants.

She stuffed her backpack with Sylvia Plath's "Bell Jar," Picoult's "The Pact," and Walsh's "The Moon Sisters." She left her copy of Shakespeare's tragedies among other accumulated volumes on the side table. Belinda swept the room with a resigned glance, tidying a pile of medical bills and letters from her physician.

She struggled to get everything into her sedan, drove to the meeting, then wrestled to set up the refreshments. She claimed her customary seat in the corner near the window. As everyone arrived, she rose with hugs and greeted them with smiles.

Mrs. Rodriguez cleared her throat. "Since everyone's here, shall we begin, ladies?"

They sat in a circle around the refreshments and flowers, books opened upon their laps. As the afternoon wore on, crumbs caught on napkins and health troubles peppered literary discussions. Lipstick left crescents of color along the rim of the insulated cups, sipping sweetened java between relevant points.

The ladies referred to and made notes in their composition books, marking important similarities in theme among the selected readings. In handwriting ranging from elaborate to meticulous, such words as 'mental breakdown,' 'inevitable declines,' and 'suicide' declared from bone-white pages the universality of depression and the equalizing factors of death.

The ladies slumped in the cushions, some fanning reddening faces, others growing pale. The conversation lagged. Mrs. Henderson's eyes slid shut, and Juliana Morcock nodded. Mrs. Rodriguez yawned, asking, "Belinda, did you only bring decaf?"

"No, there's a mixture of brews," she said. "Maybe we need more?" She filled each cup. "I'm so glad I've found like-minded people. Transitions are easier together." Her smile guarded a secret.

Mrs. Rodriguez said, "Indeed. It's delightful comradery to embark on literary journeys together. These scones are delightful. What did you put in them?"

Belinda's mysterious smile broadened, allowing partial disclosure. "The usual – flour and sugar, soda and cyanide."

By then, the effects took ahold. Belinda settled into her overstuffed chair and waited for her own consciousness to drift, knowing when the police discovered the scene, the interpretation of the notes and selected literature would indicate a suicide pact.

Haiku 17

A thousand fears call

Nothing tames the racing heart

Minds closed to small scares

Death and Taxes

The diagnosis stood. Three doctors agreed.

Inoperable.

Terminal.

Summer held no appeal. Shelagh did not feel the flower-scented breezes. She paid no mind to the children playing in the park. She replayed the medical jargon and marched through her neighborhood, angry. She had followed the rules of good health. She ate right and exercised. No smoking and only an occasional glass of wine passed her lips. Doctors predicted within a year, forty-four-year-old Shelagh would die.

She passed an old couple. He had his arm around her osteoporosis-ridden body. Shelagh had never married. A young woman pushed a pram ahead. Shelagh never bore children. She never traveled as she intended. She worked for a small paycheck, lived in a shabby apartment, and enjoyed little of her existence.

Her breath burned in her chest as she collected her mail. Bills, a circular, and a letter from the IRS. She collapsed into the sofa, avoiding its protruding spring, and ripped open the letter.

"Dear Ms. Shelagh O'Brady, Your tax refund has been deposited into your account..."

Shelagh sat up, certain her eyesight must be going. "...the amount of one million dollars and sixty-seven cents..." She rubbed her eyes and read again. Same number.

She dialed the government number listed at the top of the letter. When she reached an agent, she explained, "There is a mistake."

"We see no mistake, Ms. O'Brady."

"No, really, I don't think I've earned a million dollars in my entire lifetime, let alone earned enough to be issued such a refund."

The sound of typing proceeded the same, dispassionate response. A supervisor could find no error, either.

Shelagh hug up, baffled. Her stomach twisted, and shooting pain pressed her into the couch cushions. When it passed, she pulled herself to unsteady legs. She surveyed her home. Thrift-shop furniture. Damaged television. Leaking appliances. She sighed, speaking to the loneliness. "What a way to live."

The letter from the IRS rested atop the errant couch spring like a royal proclamation. Perhaps Shelagh's fairy godmother waved a magic wand. Instead of a ball, the edict was clear.

It might only last until midnight, but still, "Live, Cinderella."

Insomnia

What a night to give up the pills. Since Jacob left three months ago, I've not slept properly. A glass of wine takes the edge off, but the pills shut my brain up, and I sleep. When I took sleeping pills, my dreams grew wilder, more savage, so I flushed them, watched the white oblongs sink to the bottom of the toilet and slip right through that nasty hole at the bottom.

Now that the wind is howling around the house like a fiend in heat, I wonder if I open up some pipe, will I find them, those magic pills that allow my eyes to close. I lick trembling lips and pour another glass of wine. It stains the bowl of the goblet a translucent red and smells of perfumed vineyards in warmer places. The heady flavor burns as I sip. Jacob and I planned a trip to Italy and Bordeaux later in the year. Glad I didn't pay for the tickets. Who'd accompany me now, a neurotic, middle-aged insomniac growing thick around the middle, trying to mask her loneliness by pouring herself into an unappreciative workplace?

I fingered the screen on my tablet, setting the new "white noise" soundtrack to woodland sounds. No beaches. The salty surf would dredge up our last trip to the coast of Maine, before Jacob took off with his lab assistant. I'd like to say her beauty and youth enticed him, a siren song he fought but bowed to in the end. Alas, that lie must not be told. Tracy possesses few physical charms and limited mental capacities. I'm not certain how she landed the position at Labor Corp. Her only recommendations were active ovaries.

During a successful battle with cancer, I had a hysterectomy. They cut our hopes to raise a family from me. Jacob believed adopting wrong.

"If we can't raise our own, we have no business raising someone else's," he insisted.

I hit play, and cricket songs overpowered the roaring winds outside. A river rushed over rocks in a quick-moving stream.

I nestled into the bed. Though I could luxuriate anywhere across the queen sized mattress, I kept to what once qualified as "my side." His sheets remained cold and unrumpled.

From the soundtrack, little twigs broke beneath the feet of unseen woodland creatures. My eyes flew open to scan the bedroom. The wind outside my windows picked up again, rattling the fireplace doors. My heart rate increased, ears straining for unfamiliar sounds. Nothing unusual greeted me, but a feeling of being watched raised goose flesh along my arms and the back of my neck. I pressed pause, but the feeling remained. Trembling like a child after a nightmare, I clutched my blankets to my chin.

"What's wrong with me?" I wonder.

The winds died down, as though they too listened for something amiss. Eyes strained through the low light. Nothing peculiar.

Bam!

The side table Jacob used fell to the floor with a crash.

I jolted and screamed.

Nothing knocked it over, yet the table lay on its side, legs akimbo, little drawer spilling its contents upon the floor.

A medication bottle rolled to rest against the bed skirting. I reached for the amber bottle and recognized the white oblong pills. My hands shook as I struggled with the child-proofed cap. Press the bottle down against the satin sheets and turn. Ten pills. Ten nights of lucid dreams ignoring the bitter self-reproachful questions of why he left. Or one night without any cares.

I poured a last glass of wine and took all the pills and closed my eyes to the pain.

Things in the Tome

Intent upon the pages, the teens gathered around the table as Hugh opened the tome. The spine creaked like a witch's contented sigh, and the cover page revealed the book's name. "Details."

Lance said, "Where did you find this antique? I didn't think books existed any more. Burned for fuel and recycled when Multi-media chips could be injected into our arms." He pointed to his forearm.

Hugh's voice possessed a surprising richness and depth. "Thing's been locked in a trunk in our attic for a long time with Granddad's other things." He peered over his spectacles at the others, an impish grin on his face. "I've heard there is more trapped within these pressed trees and linen than mere knowledge."

Cathy's eyes sparkled like her ardor. "What do you mean?"

Greg edged closer, his arm slipping behind Cathy's shoulders. He glowered at Hugh.

Hugh shrugged. "Ever heard the phrase the Devil's in the details?"

They laughed. Cathy rested a hand on his forearm, saying,

"Oh, Hugh, you are a wealth of old-time colloquialisms."

From behind the punctuation, a primordial intelligence stirred. Titivillus stretched inky wings and scratched the type like a big cat sharpening its claws. *Get on with it, peasants.*

Dried ink flaked from the page, littering the tabletop. Cathy brushed it aside with a dismissive flick of her wrist.

Hugh cleared his throat and read aloud.

The being of the page quivered with delight. *Once you say the words, I'll be freed.* Its stomach growled with anticipation. *I've not eaten scholars in a while.*

Haiku 18

Moon friend, star buddy

Popped aboard to play a game

Planchette spears letters

Invisible Scars

Some scars are invisible.

Three-day Labor Day weekends break Kayla.

The change of the air rouses latent fears. The scent of blooming chrysanthemum and backyard barbeques inspires panic.

She scratches skin grown feverish, leaving bloody tracks. Her head pounds with remembered shame, and she battles a torrent of emotion. Anger. Fear. Revulsion. Her eyes grow wide, not seeing the world of that day, plunged into reliving an abuse that left lasting and invisible scars.

A man Kayla trusted betrayed her. When visiting her father, he violated what should have been a loving relationship.

She fought disgrace and disclosed the act to her mother, to her doctor, to any teachers who would listen. CYF sent agents. She answered their questions, ignoring the mounting stomach sickness caused by reliving. She endured forensics exams, psychological consultations, and police interviews. In the end, CYF and the state dropped charges against her violator.

She railed. "This is wrong. Why isn't he punished?"

Her mother plead with the courts to help protect her daughter. They put small safe-guards in place. With a PTSD diagnosis, she entered a weekly therapeutic program.

The strangest little things trigger reactions to unresolved memories.

These invisible scars demand acknowledgement.

Haiku 19

Welcome to waters

Inhabited w alintent

Pulled beneath the depths

Planting

Everleigh plunged the spade into the moist, spring earth. A worm peeked its wiggling pink head from its loamy home, only to be cut in half with the next spade-strike. Thrust, stomp, discard the soil, and repeat, until the hole grew despite tree-root obstacles and stones.

Her back grew tight through the shoulders and ached across her low back. Her neck throbbed, so she stretched her head left and right, up and down, hoping to ease the mounting tension. She leaned on the spade, considering the depth needed. The smell of the earth brought memories of gardening with her mother. She breathed in the plant-rich dirt offerings. Mother's Victory Garden yielded bountiful harvests year after year. Ruby sweet tomatoes, mammoth green zucchini, regal-toned eggplant, herbs, pea lines, and berries, each dug into this nutrient-enriched ground.

When she inherited, Everleigh neglected the land. The garden fell into disuse, but she determined now, this spring evening, she would renew her mother's passion.

The work of digging required more muscles than she realized, however. The exercise revealed how far from fit she'd grown. She hopped onto the turned-edged top of the shovel, forcing the head deeper into the rich, dark ground. She grunted and slung the dirt behind her before seeking a new payload.

The darkened sky sparkled with stars and a heavy, orange moon. She considered the legend that the stars were spy-holes through which the departed kept tabs on those left behind. She raised a middle finger skyward and continued. She wiped sweat from her brow with the back of a gloved hand.

Mother always required composting, insisting the plants benefited from the nutrients provided by decay. When well into her old-age, she complained that her daughter discarded her teachings.

"Mother never considered that I worked full-time and managed the house and took care of her addled self," Everleigh muttered. No child should wipe her parents' butts or ladle unappreciated soup into their toothless maws. Urine bags, Catheters, and mountains of medicines replaced candle-lit meals and theatre dates. The growing demands on her time cost her a work position as well as her social life. She put her career on hold, took a waitressing position close to home. Her new employer sympathized with her plight and scheduled around her parental obligations.

Still, Mother went on about the garden. In annoying moments of clarity, she pointed a malformed, shaking, liver-spotted finger at her daughter. "You need to plant the garden."

"But Mother, it is winter."

"Then start the seeds under light boxes, you twit."

Her father laughed, high-pitched and insane, or fell to hysterical tears.

Mother's voice grated, "If we had fresh, garden-grown vegetables, we'd be healthy," or "Go dig the root plants from under the snow. Potatoes and carrots by the flagstone."

Pausing in her progress, Everleigh considered the required depth. Mother would approve, she thought. She climbed out of the hole and uncovered her plantings. Their staring, cataract-coated eyes reflected the spy holes floating in the midnight sky. They died together, holding hands on the rented hospital beds in the living room.

Everleigh leaned close to her parents and whispered, "I'm planting the garden, Mother."

She pushed the bodies into the hole, grunting with exertion, and then covered the newest compost with the freshly-loosened, coffee-colored ground.

Paulie's Death

How dare they sport mournful visages, when theirs is the burden of responsibility for Paulie's death? Their constant taunts and merciless bullying dogged him until he made the ultimate dash to escape, mangling his body beneath speeding wheels until unrecognizable.

The mean girls who wouldn't share a "hello" let alone kindness with Paulie during his lifetime bawled in the hallways. "He was such a good person. I can't believe he's gone," they sobbed, correcting their smudged mascara before continuing to classes.

Teachers who delighted in bolstering the social order turned blind eyes to the torments.

We students had not worn down the points on our pencils when the bullies succeeded. Paulie's eyes grew dull and his voice became a mere whisper. He cried in the washroom, feet pulled up on the toilet to hide the snotty bubbles that dangled from his reddened nose.

I heard him. I wished I could comfort him, but with him as the focus, the bullies ignored me.

Tonight I visit his tombstone and I whisper, "Sorry, man. None of this shoulda happened."

Blood from my split lip collects in the corner of his freshly-carved name. A tear from my left dilutes it. The right eye is too swollen and blackened to tear up.

The wind calls through the trees like a mournful howl. I imagine Paulie behind a tree, beckoning for company. His head juts at an unnatural angle, and his smile exposes too many teeth. Gooseflesh rises, and I vomit in his floral arrangements. My jumbled insides and mangled emotions cry out.

How have they not learned their lesson? I pull a hand through my hair, finding the tender spot along the back where Bob Ikernwood slammed me into my locker. Their violence escalated since Paulie left, just as it would have if he stayed.

I play with a blade stolen from art class. It offered little protection when I was outnumbered. Now, it leaves a line and then another, each biting into my flesh. I carve my message and hope to be understood. I know the problem will not cease, but at least the school will pretend to mourn. They will find another victim, but for a few days at least, all will be quiet.

The world blurs into a thick fog, and darkness rolls in. Blood seeps from my note to mingle with the funeral flowers.

I wonder if the mean girls will dress in black, since I'm the new Paulie.

Haiku 20

Bearer of the flame

Promethius' own kin

Fire devours all

Fire Transforms

Fire's magic transforms all it touches.
Gold infuses elegance
into humble surroundings
heat warms human souls.
It dances across logs,
graceful as a sprite.
tongues send messages to heaven,
wrapped in clouds of billowing gray smoke.
Churchgoers become demonic in the flickers.
I squeeze eyes shut and whimper.
Hatred lit the blue-bright flames
that creep up my skirts.
Hair sizzles.
Skin bubbles.
Pain screeches as fragrant flesh
pops from bone
until all that remains
is unrecognizable char.
My spirit clings to the assassination spot
to admire the flame's artistry.
I'm altered,
transformed by fire's touch.

Circus Tent

Brad and Lynn set up the miniature circus tent in the center of the living room. A blue flag topped the red and yellow striped canvas cylinder. Scallops and dags dripped cheerfully, adding to the festive feel.

Adam clapped his chubby hands as he jumped and laughed. "I wuv it, Momma! Fank you, Daddy!"

Proud parents, pleased by their three-year-old's enthusiasm, grabbed hands in silent congratulations.

Adam climbed through the door flap, blue to distinguish it from the rest of the tent, and vanished from sight.

His parents knelt at the entrance.

The interior was large enough for Adam to stand. If he reached up, he could not touch the spire. Light filtered through the material cast zebra-like stripes of gold and gray. He took his peanut butter and marshmallow whip sandwich inside, chatting with imagined companions.

Brad sniffed. "I swear I smell roasted peanuts."

His wife pointed out the sandwich, raising an eyebrow. As she walked to the kitchen to tidy up the lunch dishes, he patted her rump. She giggled.

Brad caught a whiff of fresh-spun cotton candy.

"Yippee!" Adam's voice accompanied a thudding sound inside.

"I wuv horsies."

Brad tuned the television to local news, ignoring his son's boisterous exclamations. He crinkled his nose. An herbal scent, almost like the alfalfa hay Brad used to feed livestock when he was a teen, drifted through. His wife must have lit a candle.

A phrase uttered by his son registered on his distracted parental consciousness. "Uh oh, she's naked. I can't look."

The boy backed out of the tent, eyes covered with sticky hands, his tongue sticking out in a "yuck."

Brad pressed the remote's off button. "Son, what're you doing?"

"I don't want to see the naked lady, Daddy. I'm going to the baff room." The boy rushed down the hall. Under his arms was tucked a small stuffed clown doll Brad didn't recognize.

Naked lady?

Adam certainly had an active imagination. Still, Brad bent and pushed aside the blue door flap to look inside the tent.

On the canvas floor rested the plastic super hero plate, mostly-eaten sandwich and corn chip crumbs atop. Brad collected the lunch left-overs and straightened, feeling the gentle caress of the canvas against his cheek as he stood. A whiff of jasmine and sandalwood made him think of belly dancers. He closed his eye, picturing a bonfire around which swayed tanned hips barely clothed in silks and tinkling bells.

"Daddy, you're in my way."

Brad snapped out of his reverie, stepping aside to allow his son to enter.

"Did you light a fire, darling?" his wife inquired, taking the plate and kissing his flushed cheek.

"No, I thought you did."

She looked over her shoulder, head cocked to one side, but said nothing.

"I want an elephant ride!" Adam shouted.

Brad shook his head and sank into a comfortable position on his brown leather recliner and turned the new on again. Soon, he dozed and dreamed of feather and sequence-clad beauties whipping lions until they obeyed each command. He awoke, aroused.

His wife's legs stuck out of the tent's entrance. She sang a silly song with their son inside.

With a lecherous smile, Brad ran his foot up the fleshy protruding curves of her calves and thighs, wiggling his toes at the base of her pink shorts.

"Ahem, I'll be right back, Adam." Her face appeared between the tent flaps. "May I help you?"

Smile crooked across his face, he leered, wagging his finger to entice her to follow.

She sighed, disappeared once more to kiss his son loudly ("Ah, Mom!"), then emerged to grab her husband's hand. He guided her to their bedroom and lavished kisses on her eager mouth and delicate neck. She gasped and responded, met kiss with passion until they collapsed, spent and tangled in sheets no longer neatly upon their queen-sized bed.

She deposited little kisses like pops on her husband's cheeks and forehead while he admired the pert bosom jiggling beneath her white cotton t-shirt.

"Lynn, we haven't taken Adam to a circus. How do you suppose he knows so much about them?"

She stopped, eyes narrowed. "I don't know. What do you mean?"

"Well, he was talking about tigers and trained puppies and tightrope walkers. How does he even know the word trapeze?"

She laughed, shaking her head. "Adam is such a clever child." However, her brow knitted.

Adam's shrill voice interrupted the short silence that followed. "Momma? Daddy? Watch what I can do!"

Brad wondered how long Adam had stood in the bedroom doorway, but more startling were the three kitchen knives in his hands.

"I can juggle. The cwown told me I can."

Lynn reacted first, her voice quivering with concern. Her hands shook as she reached toward him. "Honey, you know you're not allowed to touch knives."

"I know, but watch. I am a circus p-former!"

The child threw the utensils into the air.

Lynn screamed.

Brad froze in horror.

Garnet splattered the white sheets and tan carpet as he attempted to catch the blades.

Aspiration Incarnate

In space, surrounded by a vast expanse of loneliness, Kyle searched for a vision. Someone with whom to converse. A friend. A lover. But he found only darkness freckled with stars. Stranded in an abandoned station, he despaired.

He dove into the vastness, intent upon drowning in the primeval cold. A song punctured his helmet. A hand illuminated the gloom. She danced into view, an aspiration incarnate. Her glow dwarfed the stars and dazzled him. He grasped her hand as a drowning man would a raft. Her intensity burned through his suit even as his desire burst his regret.

Kyle felt its presence in her gaze, the ancient cold behind her intensity, but he ignored the warning fear. Better to die in this creature's arms than live another day alone.

Trouble with Scissors

Sharon gathered the residents of the Golden Glory Senior Care Center, placing them in a semi-circle. She wheeled Mildred into the last spot. Sweet little Mildred whose eyes sparkled with laughter trapped by an unresponsive tongue patted her hand by way of thanks.

Sharon patted in return. She raised her voice to address the group. "You're going to enjoy this presentation, I think. The singer comes highly recommended."

Paulette looked up from her crocheting to scowl. "Is it another woman whose screeching is going to hurt our ears?"

Sharon laughed. "No, the singer is a man. Like I said, I've heard good things about him."

"Say, I need some scissors," Paulette said. She stretched her hand toward the Activities Aide.

Sharon rested a hand over her uniform pocket. Residents in this section were not allowed scissors. "I'm sorry, but I don't have any scissors, Paulette," Sharon lied.

Paulette muttered as she returned to her yellow yarn.

Waving from the reinforced door drew Sharon's attention. She rushed to admit the entertainer, holding the door open just long enough for the equipment to pass the threshold. The door clunked shut behind them, locking.

Set up took less than ten minutes. Sharon plugged in the

amplifiers while Mr. Melody cut the ties to allow enough cord to operate. Dressed in a tailored black suit, he imitated Tom Jones and Frank Sinatra, leaning in and singing to each resident individually. Their eyes teared up as he crooned nostalgic love songs.

Sharon's heart swelled, enjoying the pleasure of her charges.

Mr. Melody sat on the arm of Paulette's chair, sliding an arm around her thin shoulders. Her ball of yarn rolled unchecked from her lap, coming to rest in the center of the room. Her mouth popped into a surprised "O." A special light brightened her eyes, and a ruddy glow warmed her sallow complexion.

Mr. Melody crooned, bringing smiles to each resident. He slid onto the arm of Corinne's oversized chair and placed an arm around her thin shoulders. Corinne blinked in confusion. She muttered, "You're not George. Where's George?" She looked around. "Where's my husband?"

Paulette stood, an angry set to her mouth. She stooped and retrieved the yarn and threw it to her abandoned seat beside her crocheting. She stalked toward Mr. Melody, hunched and tense.

Sharon hurried toward the singer, ready to intercept his new fan. *Perhaps a dance will distract Paulette.* A shiver arrested her advance. *Are those scissors in her fist?* Sharon rushed forward. *Where would she get scissors?*

Paulette's face twisted in a snarl. The old woman said, "That's my man!"

Using her body as a shield, Sharon deflected the blow. Pain blossomed in a red stain across her uniform. A glancing blow. Not deep. Sharon wrapped her arms around Paulette's slight form, pulling the scissors from her arthritic grip.

Mr. Melody's recording continued, but he didn't sing an accompaniment. Shock froze all the residents in their comfortable chairs. Mr. Melody slid from his perch, his dropped microphone thumping against the carpeting, registering feedback. He babbled, "How'd she get my scissors? Was she going to stab me?"

"I'm sorry. I didn't mean to," Paulette said.

Sharon guided her to her room, ignoring her throbbing arm. "I know."

Haiku 21

Echoes through valleys

Clacking along decayed tracks

Phantom whistles whine

Witchery

Tia ignored her confining new accessories and threw back her head to enjoy the breeze. Its caress carried memories of her childhood, with aunts teasing her curls into fashionable braids or teaching her dance and cooking. Their remembered laughter drowned out the jeers of the assembled below her now. Her pulse quickened, and she tapped her feet on the platform, itching to join her wild-haired aunts in a whirl under a star-filled sky.

A bonfire cast the crowd into flickering shadows, transforming the good folk into nightmarish caricatures. *I wonder if they see each other for their fiendishness, or do they transfer it all on me*? Meat juices crackled as they dripped into the flames. Children clasped foil-wrapped, roasted apples, sucking cinnamon-sweet bits from sticky fingers. A hurdy-gurdy performance contributed to the air of a festival.

She whispered into the night, "If this be my stage, I stride it a queen."

A blow from behind blinded her. She lurched until the rough necklace choked.

"Quiet, Witch. No more incantations from you." She recognized the barrister's voice and understood the emotion behind the threat. She had crafted what the barrister's wife sought when she found herself saddled with an unwanted pregnancy. Herbs mixed with vinegar to make the womb reject. The barrister took umbrage and pointed an accusatory finger.

None of the good folk who had previously sought her assistance came to Tia's aid. They huddled beneath anonymity, cowards fearful of guilt by association, or they transformed their experiences into evidence for the prosecution.

"She bewitched me into drinking the slimming potion. I never sought her help. Why yes, I do look good now, don't I?"

"In my dreams she told me if I didn't pay her to minister to my cattle, they'd stop giving milk. Indeed, they were dry, so I did as the dream witch instructed."

Tia conjured images to keep her sanity when the world coalesced into a hemp hanging rope and hungry flame. With an incantation muttered under her breath, Tia summoned her mother's smiling face.

Mother fell to this threat, met this end, when she helped them, too. I should have learned that lesson instead of herb lore and medicine.

Her body ached from the tortures. Dried blood scabbed over pinpricks. Private refuges plundered with indelicate instruments.

"Confess," they yelled. She remained impassive, numbed and muted by their betrayal.

The wind's sighs drowned the swelling screams at her feet. With a crash, the trapdoor slammed beneath Tia's feet. The rope tightened, choked. Their angry faces blurred in a swirl of muddied tears until their leering ended.

Satan at the Frat Party

A pounding headache and cotton-coated mouth woke Colleen in the morning. She pushed from the cement, confused by the pentacle design and unfamiliar surroundings.

"How'd I get here?"

She pulled her rented 'Sexy Cinderella' down, noticing the rips. She struggled to a stand, then fell, her legs unsteady and unsupportive. Her insides ached.

When dressing for a party yesterday evening, her roommate Candy wore a sleek, slitted vamp getup. "Let's go, silly. Halloween won't wait."

"I don't know. Maybe I'll just study," she had said, uncomfortable in her costume and unfamiliar with frat parties.

Candy had grabbed her hands. "Absolutely not! This is going to be a great party."

Once there, Candy introduced her to a gentleman in a red suit who offered drinks. Candy took hers to join in the dance-floor fun.

Colleen sipped the deep-red drink. "Thanks. What're you dressed as?" He raised his own glass in salute.

"Myself."

The room swirled and spun.

Colleen giggled, "What's in that drink?"

He raised thick eyebrows. His mustache and goatee looked hipster.

"You're Colleen, right? Freshman?" The words plodded beneath the beat of a Metallica song.

"How'd you know?" Her voice sounded slurred. She put a shaking hand to her forehead. Thinking hurt.

He slipped a reassuring arm around her shoulder. She closed her eyes, unsure why she felt comforted.

She jolted to the here and now, stinking like fish and feeling bruised. She threw up, sobbing between each heave. She wiped her tears, finding it hard to breath. Her insides lurched as she realized she could only identify her attacker as "Satan at the frat party."

Smell of Souls

My stomach aches and I tremble, a weakened mess of nerves and hysteria, reduced to trembling knees, itching skin, and tears. I search for an escape but spy none. I wonder, "Where's that famous window, since every door's closed." I suppose I could simply fail, but failure's never been an option.

I give myself a pep-talk, hearing the mania even in my inner voice. "Just get it over with. You'll survive. Really. You always do."

She stands when I enter, her chair tipping to a clattering rest on the floor. "No, get out. I know who you are and why you're here. I'm not going, not ready!" Her voice reaches a soprano crescendo as she backs away.

I stretch out a shaking hand toward her, a reassurance against her concern. "I'm not here to hurt you."

She waves a pool stick in front of her. "Don't lie. I smell the death on you."

I smelled it too, a rot dripping from my pores. My quaking increases. No doors. No windows. Trapped in this booze-scented hell, I know the only way out is through. I snatch the cue stick from her grasp and close. "I'm sorry about this."

Her ineffectual fists pound against my chest, bruising my broken heart. Her shrill screams pierce my eardrums until tears coat my cheeks. Their pitch hurts. I cover her mouth and sink through her lips until the sound chokes, sputters, and falls silent.

Her shocked eyes accuse from disassembled stardust and clay until she hears the music. Lights glisten along a pathway only she can follow, leaving me to wait alone in the darkened pool hall. With her departure, a smell of orange blossoms lingers for just a minute. My job never grows easier. Instead of becoming numb to their protests, I concentrate on the deconstruction and the smell of their souls.

My fingers dance through where once she stood, trying to capture a bit of her freshness, but only decay perfumes my soul. My vomit splashes my feet and absorbs back into my essence, adding to the resultant stink. Her corpse's sightless stare accuses.

My legs buoy up, and my breathing returns to normal. No more crying. No more weakness, at least not until next time.

Someone aglow with health enters, screams, and backs away. He dials the report with trembling voice.

"I don't know what happened, but dear God! I think she's dead." He stares, shocked, at the husk, never noticing the fading scent of oranges or my pervasive rot.

There are no windows for me, no streams of rescuing light nor even shadows transformed into hulking beasts. I know better than check for a door. Instead, I rack the balls in their triangle, unseen, and await my next assignment.

Frigid

I'm freezing. I climb into bed, grateful for the heavy comforter and cotton top sheet. I tuck my chin, nestling into the warmth, but the shivering won't stop. He's asleep, but if I move slowly I shouldn't disturb him.

His snores sound like a big cat's purrs. I reach around his girth. It has grown since marriage. Nestling my head between his shoulder blades, I snake my feet behind his knees. He smells familiar, like home, a mixture of kitchen spices and a man's musk. I sigh, breathing in the comfort.

He shivers, but I remain still.

"Brr, it's frigid in here!" He pulls the blanket to the stubble on his chin.

A soft, soprano voice answers. "You're shaking, honey. Are you okay?"

Wait, we're not alone in this bed! The thought chills me, and my grip tightens.

She throws her arm around him, brushing my hair as her fingers pass.

It's getting a bit crowded on this queen-sized mattress.

Though reluctant, I ease my way out of the bed, casting a last, longing look at its emanating warmth.

"What was that breeze?" It shook the bed," she said.

He nestled closer to his new wife's thin body, apparently grateful for her warmth after feeling my embrace from the grave.

Perfume, Pasties, and a Smile

Antoinette wiped baby oil over her body. The sheen accented curves and definition, and although it blocked her pores and caused her to sweat, it also disguised perspiration.

Nobody found a sweaty stripper attractive, she thought.

Tasseled pasties and jeweled thong in place, she layered sexy silks and sprayed glitter into her hair. She defined her dark eyes with heavy, Egyptian-inspired makeup and spritzed on fruity perfume. She climbed to her place, ready for her grand entrance.

Last of all, she stepped into glittering, spiked heels.

She didn't set out to become an exotic dancer, but she was good at it and made killer tips.

An appreciative roar of cat calls from the drunken clientele announced, "Show time."

Antoinette slipped from the rafters and slid down a crimson ribbon. The effect made her skirts billow like a sunset cloud to the stage. She serpentined and shimmied, peeling layer after layer as though plucking petals from a daisy. The silk drifted to the stage, soft as webs.

The once-rowdy crowd grew enraptured, mouths and eyes wide and hungry. They offered money for her nearness and threw roses on the stage. She crushed the blooms beneath her stilettos and knelt before one lucky audience member. His hungry gaze swept her nubile form, and a lecherous grin crossed his wolfish features. He folded a bill with Benjamin Franklin's portrait and slid it into her sparkling strap just above the hip bone.

"Tonight," he yelled.

She blinked like a school girl, fingers to her coy lips. "Tonight?" she mouthed.

She continued her dance until all the layers of her costume piled like a cocoon at the back of the stage, and when she took her bow, all she wore were heels, pasties, perfume, and a smile.

The crowd erupted with pleasure.

She climbed her silk cord for her exit as the stage hand gathered her costume.

The next girl took the stage, and the men hooted and yelled as she swirled around a phallic pole.

Antoinette removed her heels and descended from the rafters. No sooner had her bare feet hit the wood than "Mr. Benjamin Wolfgrin" appeared.

She smiled up at him. "I guess by later you mean now?"

Desire danced in his eyes, and his lecherous smile and

raised eyebrows broadcasted his intentions. He reached for her.

She stepped back, naked but for her g-string and pasties.

"Can't you give a girl a second to catch her breath?"

He lunged. His huge hands felt rough against her skin.

She dropped to her knees. Slippery with oil and sweat, she escaped his embrace. With a lithe movement, she darted out the stage door into the dark alley.

He followed, and with a slam, the metal door locked them out.

Cool night air rose gooseflesh along her naked skin. She clutched her heels to her bosom.

"What's your plan then, Mister? Get me all alone in a dark alley? Hardly seems like a gentlemanly move to me."

A toothy grin split his face. "I'm no gentleman, and you're no lady." To make his intentions clear, he pulled at the zipper of his pants.

Antoinette stepped away, deeper into the shadows. The stage music muffled the further into the alley she went, but so would any screams.

"Oh no you don't." He used his greater height to his advantage and reached for her.

She side-stepped over a mound of molding clothes to avoid his touch.

His brow lowered. "I paid for it."

"You paid to watch me dance. Now leave before someone gets hurt."

The man shook his head like an enraged bull. "You little…"

Before he leveled his insult, she leapt, lithe as a cat. She landed atop his shoulders and slammed the metal heel of her stilettos into his eye sockets.

The man bellowed with rage and pain, clawing at his eyes.

She landed beside her blinded, would-be attacker.

He pulled the shoes from their sticking places. Gore dripped from his ruined eyes. "I'll kill you! I'll kill you!"

"You've gotta catch me first." She skipped around him, touching with her fingertips to taunt him.

He caught a hank full of hair and yanked.

She laughed as the false tresses fell loose in his grasp.

He couldn't see her transformation. Still beautiful, still naked, Antoinette shimmered in the dingy low light of the alley. As she exerted herself, her shimmer intensified to a glow. Soon, the alley sparkled with mischief.

She drew her polished fingernails across his chest, leaving gashes with each passage. She licked his shoulder. Where her tongue touched, an angry welt rose.

He windmilled his arms and made contact.

Her light flickered when she said, "oof." She pouted out of his reach. "I thought you wanted to play."

He kicked toward the sound of her voice.

She avoided him with ease. "No playing then? Okay."

She laughed, head tilted toward the inky sky. Her mouth expanded and exposed five rows of glass and metal shards stuffed into her impossible jaw. She vaulted to his shoulders and wrapped her legs about his throat. As he scratched and clawed for air, she clamped her mouth on his face in a final and deadly kiss. She excreted acid that ate him from the inside out.

Within minutes, he fell among the other discarded clothing behind the dumpster. Not even his skeleton remained.

Antoinette licked gore from beneath her fingernails, her mouth restored to its human disguise.

She straightened her g-string and wiped optic nerve from her heels.

After all, nobody liked an untidy stripper.

Holding His Tongue

They act as though everything's normal, like there wasn't a man bleeding out on the kitchen floor last night. My mother and big brother pour bowls of cereal and slather butter on toast and ignore the searing, antiseptic stench of bleach. My eyes water, though, and not only from the sodium hypochlorite. In my mind, I still see his life traced out in the cracks of the tile, stained in my mind despite the thorough cleaning.

They had handed me a mop and no choice.

"We did this for you," they had yelled.

But I hadn't invited the monster to slither from beneath the bed.

My mother did. In fact, she married him.

I rub my complaining stomach.

Mother strokes my hair. "You have to keep up your strength, sweetheart. Eat something."

But I can't. The idea of cereal doesn't agree with me. Its chunks resemble clots. The milk pours corpse pale.

I kneel over the waste bin and vomit until I'm hollowed, but I'm not. Not entirely. Inside me, something grows. Pushes. Leeches what it needs from me.

It is this something that dictated the death. He created the something when he pulled off his mask and revealed not a loving stepfather but a monster intent on pedophilia. He invaded my room, pushed into my bed, defiled my body, and left me with these abdominal pain and lasting repercussions.

A knock at the front door startles me, and with a yip, I drop my bowl. It shatters, much like my stepfather's skull when they surprised him last night. He thought he could slither into his hidey hole in my bedroom, but my brother flushed him out with a wire-wrapped baseball bat. Big bro's a part of the minors, but they'll be calling him up any time now, especially with the intense practice he gives his swing. He chased that snake into my mother's waiting cleaver. Mom knows the value of good and sharp implements, and she's an expert in their use.

When he reached for me and begged for his life, what grew inside me revolted. Furious, I knelt at his ruined face, reached into his gawking mouth, and pulled out his lying tongue. It resisted, but with a foot placed on his cheek and a fall onto my bottom, I managed. It pulsed in my grip, moist and warm, the perfect definition of him condensed into a single part.

Before my brother answers the door, he winks a reassurance. Mom rubs her hand up my back and works at a knot in my shoulder. My family loves me. I know. I feel their devotion just as surely as oxygen fills my lungs with each breath. When they discovered the treachery, their reaction was immediate. Like a well-oiled machine, we worked in tandem to destroy and dispatch. Other than an odor, nothing remained of the ill-doer. Nothing upon us indicated guilt except my evil step-father's tongue stilled and stifled in my pocket.

The door opens to a morning so bright, no nighttime fracas could be bad enough to have darkened it. A police officer smiles at us and removes his hat.

"Good morning, folks. I'm here to investigate a report of some strange sounds last night."

Mother offers coffee. "We had a fight, and my husband left."

He accepts the steaming cup. "Any idea where he's off to or when he'll be back?"

Mother shrugs. "Not sure. Said something about Mexico, I think."

My brother nods.

I squeeze my fist around the souvenir in my pocket to fight nausea. It squelches a bit beneath my grip but keeps as silent as a secret.

Trouble in a Teacup

My teacup clattered in my trembling hand when I had realized. I scowled into its amber depths, the tempest in the teacup, and had willed my breathing to calm. "You'll give yourself away, fool. There's no tell-tale heart beneath that board," I had thought.

Yet, I knew there was.

I had pressed my lips into a line when the lead officer took another swallow from his own china. I had made a grave error. I studied the eyes of the officers before me and presented my best smile, the endearing grin that earned me posts within the PTA and garnered the trust of children.

Their pupils showed the effects. I had used the wrong sweetener, the one I reserved for plump cherubs with the sweetest meat, children who delighted as the crystals crackled like fairy chimes when dropped into a cup of chamomile.

"Imported from Germany," I had explained as they drowsed in the comfortable chairs with lavender-scented pillows. Their lids had slid to rest upon flushed cheeks, easing the butchery.

Adults like these grown men tasted gamey. What could I do with these two? They outweighed me, so disposing of them in the basement would be impractical, and they parked their vehicle outside. If they woke, they'd overpower me. Besides, police phoned in their whereabouts.

As their chins drooped to their uniformed chests, I covered them each with a crocheted afghan. I would have to hurry. They were certain to suspect they were drugged.

I had packed, starting with filling the cooler. Leaving such hard-earned delicacies as fresh child-meat was not an option. I had thrown together what remaining possessions I could, sighing over what must be left behind.

When the officers woke, I would be gone.

Haiku 22

Burst from carrion

A Phoenix born of black wings

Queen Morrigan reigns

Their Baby

Let me begin by explaining that this is no ordinary tale related by an ordinary child, though none around me are observant enough to realize this. They coo and gurgle at me as if I were a mortal infant, ignoring the truth.

It is certainly no easy task to be born, neither for the mother nor for the child. I suppose it is difficult, too, for those who have a stake in the outcome, but theirs seems rather an inconsequential agony after those endured by us two in the delivery room. Then again, I have never been one for sentimentality, knowing that empathy is an utterly useless weakness.

Thus, after the arduous journey down a restrictive passage out of an incomprehensively small exit, I lay on a table beneath, of all things, a sun lamp.

The fools!

I tried to berate their ignorance, only to find that words were beyond my capacity, with only the caterwauling of infancy forming in my swollen throat. Since even simple motor control escaped me, I screwed my eyes tightly shut and wailed like a banshee that I once knew.

Swaddled tighter than a corpse in a shroud, I was presented to the woman who carried me inside of her body for forty weeks. Is it not ironic, the usage of the number forty? Divinity has its jokes.

As does fate, apparently.

The woman offered sustenance to me, nearly smothering me with engorged mammary parts. The temptation to simply bite there and then, to feed properly, was very strong, but something akin to gratitude prevented me. This woman would never again have a girlish figure, since I did my best to push as much room for myself within her as was possible. The stretch marks would live on her skin as snaking reminders of the role that she played this autumn evening. Hers was the blood that sustained me through gestation, and a feeling almost of comradery filled my conscience. Whatever was I doing with one of those?

"We will send a lactation consultant, dear." A cloying voice from the nurse Kozinski comforted the teary-eyed, exhausted woman who looked with evident concern at me.

I opened my mouth by way of explanation but could only cry when incomprehension was evident within her maternally bovine eyes.

Another, named Harris, took me to a room where my weight and height were announced at 9 pounds 6 ounces and twenty-one inches in length.

"Big baby," one observed while slinging me about like a mere doll.

As the day in the hospital progressed, enduring indignities better left unvoiced, visitors came. Relatives of the mare and stud commented on imagined similarities in appearances between us.

"His are the palest blue eyes!" many would squeal amid my protesting wailing.

"Of course they are, fools." I screamed in my mind. Had none of them even imagined the eyes of death? My list of forage grew with their every inane comment.

Mercifully, the bouquets and baskets brought into the tiny room were devoid of roses. Carnations and their ilk could only lend an almost funeral quality to the place, not add to my considerable discomfort.

It was then that the quack discovered my teeth.

Instead of the inspired dread that should have filled the fools, the entire hospital staff gathered around as I writhed in pain beneath that unwholesome light, pointing and commenting about the "oddness." Jennings, Lawrence, and Kozinski their names were. I marked them well, and my memory is longer than any mortal life.

However, the food thrust upon me was utterly unpalatable, and I expelled it with conviction. Colic was mentioned in quietly consoling tones to the anxious parent. Many folk remedies were mentioned, from pressure on the stomach to coral beads. Modern remedies such as mildly medicinal drops, also, were mentioned, though they seemed rather a last resort.

So modern man did still hold some of the old beliefs. They simply stopped reading the correct books to obtain the necessary information. Knowledge of folk remedies, after all, is far less important than knowing of that which could undo any cure.

When I grew, I would tell them, if I did not eat them first.

Practically, I could not feed around so many since I hadn't any motor control, ineffectual feeding at best. Patience I must have, though the hunger was unbearable.

Dread, however, and not patience came to me.

These people did not know what they did, that my torture was sealed by their silvery instrument.

I still am hungry and will be for a very long, it seems, since infant teeth grow slowly, four months at the earliest according to the woman's infant book. The cruel irony was brought by a dentist who removed my fangs before I could move to feed.

Freedom Pie

Few claim baking at midnight as an eccentricity, but I do. I specialize in pies. Pumpkin's my favorite. I love the feel of pulp mixed with spices squelching through my fingers. Father got himself into quite a huff over my nocturnal activities. "Unnatural," he said, pointing a nicotine-stained finger in my face. I'd smile, because once he'd slept off the drink, he'd tuck in, sometimes devouring the whole thing without sharing.

I expect he'll be hungry. Always is after a night of cards, so I mixed in an extra-special spice just for him, a little untraceable something I'll call free-at-last.

Drawn

Although dust coated the brown wings, the fuzz of the moth on the light pole intrigued her. I ran a finger along its plump body.

Hmm, rougher than I thought.

The insect lifted from the wall and fluttered in erratic arcs around the streetlight. Its shadow speckled the ground near her hem.

I remember when these were flaming gaslights.

At each bay of light, insects bobbed like popcorn, drawn through the gloom.

Just like me.

I pulled the hood of my cloak over my brow and replaced the kid glove I'd removed to stroke the moth. Fog curled from the river, reaching to engulf my ankles. Walking on a cloud. Each step sent the fog rolling. Riverboats sounded mournful blasts made eerie by the nighttime.

On every porch glowed a jack-o-lantern. I glared at a grinning gourd.

I chose this neighborhood because of its aged community. From whence comes the abundant Halloween spirit?

I shivered, pulling the fabric tighter about my neck.

Where's my welcoming glow, my unattended household? We walkers can't enter where a jack -o-lantern watches. Stupid, age-old rules.

A pack of children rushed along the roadside. One stopped, her weighted sack soiled from dragging. She backed away from me until she found her mother's hand.

"Momma," she said, "do you see the ghost?"

The mother's gaze followed where the child pointed, but she blinked, unable to see. She ruffled the girl's hair.

"It's just your imagination, honey."

I smiled at the child, revealing needle-sharp teeth.

The girl screamed and buried her face in her mother's side.

"Let's get out of here! Please, Momma."

After casting a last blind search for her daughter's assailant, the mother guided her child along until their slight forms became engulfed by thickening fogs.

I tidied my Gibson-girl hairdo and straightened my hat. Often the young recognized my otherworldliness, but I was no ghost. No, much more than spirits strolled the streets when the veil thinned on the night of All Hallow's Eve.

Vinegar and Brown Paper

Audrey scowled at the state of the antique mirror, the sole item she inherited from her Aunt's vast estate. Greedy relatives who spent little time with Auntie when she lived seized everything else from her two houses and their holdings. Audrey knew their true nature. They called her a spinster, stigmatized her introversion, but when they saw her, they smiled with saccharine sweetness. Before retiring, she'd spent most of her adult years teaching elementary school, and she recognized disdain.

Audrey blew across the glass surface, sending a puff of decay eddying through her entry hall. Dust coated the surfaces and encrusted the ornate frame's botanical carvings. She swiped it with a soft cloth, revealing silver gilt. Her arthritic fingers complained as she winkled grime from the carved flowers, restoring the glory of the frame.

Through hard work and determination, Auntie had accumulated her fortune. Audrey had admired her grit and fire and called Auntie her role model. Neither woman married. Romantic entanglements complicated and stifled. While Audrey settled into a comfortable situation as principal at a prestigious private boarding school, Auntie held the deed to the property. Auntie invested her money with an almost supernatural wisdom, making money with each purchase and sale.

Audrey frowned at the frame. Some silver wore from the right corner, but considering the age of the piece, that was to be expected. No chips marred the glass, but discoloration fogged the bottom.

Audrey's own reflection scowled, displaying the ravages of a bitter old age. Frown lines etched deep between her brow and a pinched, thin-lipped countenance unaccustomed to smiles, her own or gifted by others toward her. Still, her back remained ram-rod straight, a testimony to years of self-inflicted discipline and an almost Spartan determination to imbue future generations with unswerving work ethics. With each graduating class, Audrey observed in her pupils a growing sense of entitlement and disregard for rules and personal responsibility. She took the school board's request for her resignation as a sign of changing times. Audrey, like her philanthropic Auntie, were vestiges of better times.

She wadded brown paper and spritzed it with vinegar to shine the mirror. No new-fangled products for this antique. As expected, the first pass swirled the grime. The second presented an unmuddied top but a mottled bottom image with child-sized handprints creeping along the lower frame. Auntie hadn't any children, but undoubtedly these oily marks resulted from negligent relatives showing no regard for the antics of their unruly progeny. Audrey imagined their grubby mitts befouling her only inheritance while their parents distributed Auntie's silver, china, and jewelry.

No amount of elbow grease released the phantom hands. In fact, they increased in number with Audrey's ministrations. The giggles of neighbor children skipping rope down the street annoyed her as she scrubbed. The sound punctuated the appearance of new miniature hands. Audrey discarded the soaked paper and ground her teeth. They would not win, these interlopers marking her only physical remembrance from her beloved Auntie. Auntie had taught her to persist. She insisted on perfection and would have punished Audrey severely for any half-hearted efforts.

The neighbors' taunting laughter wafted in with a summer breeze as Audrey strained to remove the vestiges of childish impropriety from the mirror. Her face pinched inward. "Darned kids and their unthinking parents," she muttered, redoubling her efforts. She imagined using her trusty wooden ruler to slap their hands away from her possession as she'd done as a teacher. As a principal, she'd used her authority to greater effect, telling the children to drop their drawers and bend before the class to receive punishments, just as she'd been disciplined by Auntie through her formative years. Learning consequences early provided a firm foundation for the straight-and-narrow life. Her school turned out no juvenile delinquents.

"There," she said, stepping back to appreciate her handiwork. The silver glittered like a rich old lady's hair, but from her new vantage, Audrey saw missed handprints.

Tears blurred her vision as she applied extra elbow grease to the growing collage of child's hands. They seemed to scratch the other side of the mirror, and infernal titters persisted outside.

As she had continued in her position at the school, parents protested her measures. She remained unyielding, though she heard the complaints. Subsequent generations clung to an attitude of neglect her upbringing couldn't abide. In fact, her wish to instill and maintain appreciation for learning and restraint drove her along her career path. Audrey recognized her adherence to tradition as a continuation of the pioneering spirit that made her country great.

A lump rose in her throat as she remembered the reddened faces of miscreant students, eyes brimming with accusation. She admonished the handprints, her reflection, and the specter of her overbearing Auntie. "I never meant to hurt them. Just wanted them to be the best they could. Like I was taught."

Her reflection mocked her, trapped in a prison of self-imposed blame. Wrinkles formed prison cells around her features. She questioned her motivations and recognized a lifetime of cruelty within her eyes.

She rested her forehead against the glass, heedless of the resulting smudge. One handprint stood out, clear and centered. She covered it with her gnarled fingers. Her wizened skin hid her shame. She balled a fist and struck at memories, shattering her only inheritance from Auntie.

Haiku 23

It sprouts from sorrows

Nourished by turmoil and guilt

Tears souls limb from limb

Quietly, Ross

It waited in Ross's closet as it did most nights, hidden from the light, its steely nails scratching even during the brightest of afternoons. At night, the door made a slow, high-pitched screech and it scuffled out, red eyes glowing. Moonlight glinted off the strong, sharp teeth. Its snake-like tail whispered behind its plump, gray body.

Ross huddled under the covers, praying for protection. His brow gleamed with sweat in the golden half-light of the smiley face night light. His hands ached from clutching the covers to his chin. He dared not cry out. It would know he was awake if he screamed.

Ross held his breath. It came closer, its pin sharp claws catching on the bedding as it climbed. He ducked under the covers, a cocoon of sanctuary. He felt the thing's weight pressing on his chest as it scurried toward his face. He hunched his shoulders and drew up his knees, hoping his smallness might escape notice.

He heard sniffling sounds, felt the thing digging at his covers. He quaked and tightened his grip on the rough cotton blankets. He held the blanket taut, his only defense against the invader his parents refused to believe existed. Ringing deafened his right ear. His ear always rang when the thing drew close. It squeaked. Ross pressed his trembling lips together to keep from answering in kind.

The pressure changed on the bed and a thump announced that it was on the ground, scampering among his playthings, hiding in baskets, chewing beloved books. Ross released a breath he hadn't known he'd held. He shook with terror.

Why won't mom and dad believe me? I'm so scared.

He whimpered and waited for morning to brighten his room and chase the rodent back to the closet where it nested in the back wall.

###

When the alarm sounded, Ross sighed. He nestled into the comforts of his bed. With daybreak, he could sleep without fear of the rat.

"Time to get up! Get dressed."

"Please, I'm so tired." Terrifying evenings exacted a toll. He felt queasy, unsteady.

"Up," said his father, annoyance reverberating through his deep voice.

Ross groaned. When he reached for his clothes, he stumbled. Dizziness overtook him, and he careened like a drunken pirate into the edge of his desk. "Argh!"

"Come on, chum, suck it up. We have to get you to Uncle Tim's. We're going to be late for work if we don't go soon."

Ross whimpered but got ready, nursing the growing bump on the back of his head.

###

Uncle Tim moved using a wheelchair. He watched Ross during workdays when school was out. He had wild hair, wise eyes, and a smile reluctant to intrude on Ross's pervasive melancholy.

"Hey, Ross Sauce," Uncle Tim greeted.

Ross fist bumped, then retired to a customary corner of a dark, stained couch to read the latest "American Heroes" comic. The tiny black letters swam before his eyes, and Ross fell asleep.

"Wake up, Ross." Uncle Tim shook his shoulders, fingers digging with insistence.

Ross propped himself up. His comic slipped to the shag carpet. Ross rubbed the sleep sand from his eyes with trembling hands. His temples pounded, his heart raced, and it hurt to move his eyes. The air cooled the sweat that dripped from his hairline.

Uncle Tim leaned as far from his chair as he could without falling. He stared with red-rimmed eyes at his nephew. "Dude, what the hell was that? You scared the – are you okay now?"

Ross licked his cracked lips. "I'm okay. What happened?"

Uncle Tim relaxed, but his gaze never left his nephew's face. "Beats me, but that was some trip, kid." He reached into the pocket of his black leather vest for a pack of cigarettes. Uncle Tim's hands shook as he took a drag, exhaling smoke like a dragon. He tipped his head to the right, scrutinizing the boy. He blinked, rapid repetitions like gunfire, then asked, "You want to talk about it?"

Ross cleared his throat. He refused to burden his uncle. "No. I just want a drink."

"Bet you do," Uncle Tim muttered and nodded. He tousled Ross's hair. Cigarette smoke snaked around the two.

"You know the soda's in the fridge."

That evening, Ross delayed the inevitable by dragging out evening rituals. Teeth shone from the ministrations of paste and floss. Shower, comb hair, lay out clothes for the morning showed him a responsible man of ten, even if it was only an illusion.

"What on earth are you doing now, son?" asked his mother.

"Just tidying up my room."

"It is bed time now. Get to sleep."

He bit his lip, trembling. His heart raced faster as his mind searched for an escape. He ran his hand across his smooth chin.

I need a distraction. What will work on Mom?

"Mom, do you think a girl will ever like me?"

She sat on his bed, a mother behind beautiful, brown eyes. "Of course, honey. Why would you worry about such things?"

He shrugged his shoulders, fighting an urge to close heavy eyes. If he gave in, she would leave. He did not want to be left.

She put a hand beneath his chin and looked into his eyes.

"You are so handsome, with your father's strong jaw line and your grandmother's dark hair." She studied his face, concern playing with the crow's feet at the corners of her eyes. "You haven't been sleeping again, have you?"

He was too tired to deny the truth.

"Please tell me what is bothering you."

A shiver ripped up his spine like an electrical impulse. He stole a glance at the closet, then begged his mother, "Not in here. Can we talk in the other room, please?"

Her mouth pinched in, as though blocking words. She traced a hand along the side of his face and nodded. "Just for a couple of minutes though."

He bolted from the room, closing his door behind them.

"I told you, there's a rat in the closet in that room," he whispered as they hurried to the sofa.

She embraced him. "Honey, I love you so much, and I know that you are scared, but please listen to reason. There is no rat. I had an exterminator inspect the entire house. There are no rodents at all. Not even a mouse or hamster."

He shrugged out of her hug. "He must've missed it, Mom. The thing comes out every night. It climbs on my bed and sits on my chest. It is huge and disgusting."

She looked ceiling-ward, as though patience might fall like manna from the heights. "Ross, honey, I don't know what to tell you."

"Maybe it hid in the wall?"

Her lips pressed into a thin line, and swollen eyelids veiled concerned eyes. She took a steadying breath before continuing in a level voice. "I had them check the walls, love. No rat."

Mom would not help. His neck and shoulders stiffened, and his ears rang. "I'm not making this up."

"You've always been imaginative, my love. You probably dreamed it." She hugged him. "Now please get some sleep."

He lowered his chin and closed his eyes to think. He willed an emerging headache away.

I need a plan.

He nodded off on the couch beside his mother.

"Go to sleep. You are so tired that you're falling asleep here."

"Hey, that's a great idea! Can I sleep here tonight? Please mom?"

Her breath huffed in a frustrated sigh. "Fine, just for the love of all, go to sleep."

"Can you get my pillows for me, please?"

"Seriously?"

"Never mind. Just stay here while I get them."

He retrieved his blanket and pillow.

She tucked him in with a kiss on the forehead and smiled. "I've not done that in a long time." She pushed his hair back from his cheek. "Don't forget to say your prayers, darling."

He nodded, though he'd not prayed since the rat started haunting his dreams a couple of weeks earlier.

Ross knew his parents disliked night-time disturbances. He followed rules, comfortable with their structure. If he did something wrong, acted out, he punished himself with guilt and confessed for relief. Breaking this rule drained him, but terror gripped him, and he did not know what else to do.

Lack of sleep hurt his eyes and made them look puffy. His appetite disappeared and so did his waist. His clothes hung on him like hand-me-downs. His dark hair defied efforts of control, springing skyward like an indomitable spirit.

He rubbed his chin, a calming technique from his early childhood. He steeled himself before turning the handle to his parents' room.

He whispered, "Mom, Mom, please wake up. I am so scared and don't know what to do."

She stirred.

"Please, Mom, I need you."

"Ross," her voice sounded rough, as though dredged from a gravel pit. "This needs to stop."

Desperation inspired his words. He quaked with reaction, sick to his stomach, exhausted but terrified to sleep. "I know. I do." He fought tears that collected in a lump high in his throat. The pressure in his head pushed at his eyes from their sockets.

She sat up with a grunt. She swung her feet from the covers to waiting slippers and grabbed a soft pink robe draped across her slipper chair. She cast an envious glance at his sleeping father, then grabbed her son's hand and pulled him from the bedroom.

In the living room, she yawned. "What is it now, son?"

"The rat," he hissed. "It came into the hallway."

Her eyes narrowed. "Where is it now?"

"I don't know. I heard it scuffling along, so I ran."

She looked around at the glare of every lamp in the room. She turned one off, then another.

"What are you doing?" His voice pitched high in hysteria.

"You can't sleep with all of these lights on, and we both need

- 202 -

sleep."

"Please, Mom, leave them on."

She stopped, hand outstretched toward a desk lamp. "Why?"

"It doesn't like the light, I think."

Her arm dropped with a *smack* to her side. She shook her head, and frowned. "Fine. One light on, but you have to go to sleep."

He nodded, staring down the hallway led to his room. His voice sounded small when he said, "Mom, why won't it leave me alone?"

She sat beside him and looked down the hall as well. Worry trumped tired, he guessed. He put his arm around her shoulders and inhaled the homey scent of furniture polish and face soap. She hummed a tune from cradle days when sleep brought dreams of adventures. Her warmth and nearness comforted him, and he slept at last.

###

The morning brought the usual rush for readiness. Hurried breakfast, hasty preparations, and then he dashed to catch the school bus. As he ran out the door, he overheard his father say, "You need to stop babying him. No more sleeping on the couch. Got it?"

On the school bus, he rested his head against the cool, smudged glass for the trip and thought. His headache felt better since he managed to sleep.

School bored him, but he earned good grades. He'd become quiet and reserved since the rat began its night time visits. He drifted to sleep, head pillowed on hands, at his desk at times. At recess, Tammy Hanson and the Pepper twins ran screaming from a corner of the fenced exercise yard. A group of boys investigated the area. Ross tagged along. "Ewww, what is that thing?" Bob O'Malley asked.

Jake Simsick grabbed a stick and poked at the brown fur. Ross edged closer, peering between the boys' shoulders. The animal wiggled independent of the prodding. "Uughh!" Jake dropped the stick and backed away.

Ross retrieved the wood and touched it to the rodent, turning it onto its feet.

"It is a rat," he exclaimed. The boys moved closer, following his lead. The thing squeaked. Ross' shoulders twitched. His stomach knotted. With a quick thrust, he speared it. The animal squeaked again and slowly turned beady dark eyes. Ross felt ill. He raised the stick again and smacked the rat on its shoulder, its stomach, and its rump. He continued, tears streaming down his face.

The boys around him muttered, but Ross remained in his own world. Only the rat mattered. His ears rang. He sneered, smashing it with his stick until a teacher pulled him away.

She took the stick and threw it over the fence. Kneeling before him, she smoothed Ross' hair and wiped his tears. "Are you okay, Ross?" Her voice sounded as though it traveled through a heavy, spring fog. "Come on, let's get you to the nurse."

He lay on a cot with a thermometer under his tongue, wrapped in a scratchy olive-green blanket. The teacher and nurse conferred behind a screen. Their words sounded like bees buzzing. He closed his eyes. The ringing in his ears brought the headache back. His neck and shoulders stiffened and cramped. *How many times did I hit that thing?*

The nurse removed the thermometer and checked the reading. "That looks normal." Ross knew his temperature was the only thing the nurse found "normal" about Ross. He closed his eyes and slept until his mother collected him.

###

He came home from school and bounced his backpack onto his bed. He froze when he noticed the open closet door.

"Mom!" he yelled, backing out.

He startled when she touched his shoulders. "Who's been in my room?"

"Me. Come see."

He remained in the hall until she grabbed his hand and pulled him along.

"I sorted out your toys and clothes. It is all much more organized. But best of all, I've re-paneled everything with cedar board. No rat holes. No rats." She straightened a shirt, the hangars tinkling like wind chimes. Her satisfied look froze when she saw his face. "Honey, are you alright?"

Why can't she see it?

The rat hunched on a shelf just behind his mother's head, between a box labeled "puzzles" in his mother's handwriting and his junior chemistry kit. It stretched its mouth open, revealing startling, sharp white teeth. Its red eyes glowed, pupil-less, like Hell's embers.

"Mom, turn around."

She looked over her shoulder at her handiwork. "What? What is wrong?"

"There, on the shelf at eye-level, do you see anything – weird?"

He gleaned from her blank expression she saw nothing but a well-organized space.

Am I crazy?

He felt faint. "Mom, I think I need help!" He turned and ran to the bathroom and vomited.

He overheard his mother talking, voice a high-pitched whisper, into her cellular telephone. "Tim, I'm just so worried about him. Oh, would you please? I think that would help. Thank you! You are the best big brother!" She paced with irregular strides, her limp evident in agitation. "We can try. Why don't you come for dinner? Great! I will see you at six, okay? Thanks again! I love you!"

She slumped into a kitchen chair.

"Mom?"

She jumped. "Ross, I didn't know you were there." She hesitated before asking, "How are you feeling?"

"Fine. Is Uncle Tim coming to dinner?"

She nodded.

"Good."

Ross suspected it was time he confided in Uncle Tim.

He completed his math homework, then helped with dinner preparations. He chopped onions, wiping tears from his eyes.

"Run the onion under the water. That will take away some of the oils that make you tear up."

He did. Mom sliced mushrooms and dropped them in a red-wine sauce. The kitchen filled with good smells. Popovers baked. Meat broiled. Ross's stomach rumbled, anticipating the meal.

"Set the table, love. Use the good plates."

"Okay, Mom."

He placed the china, the silver clanked atop the linen napkins. He lit the white candle centerpiece and washed up for the meal. When he took his place, Uncle Tim sat opposite him. They enjoyed the meal, and then Ross helped his mom tidy up after.

"Why don't you chat with Uncle Tim?" she suggested. "Show him your room."

Ross shifted his weight from leg to leg and reached for his chin. "Okay," he said.

Uncle Tim wheeled into Ross's room. He looked around. "Mighty neat for a boy's room," he said. He perused the titles on the bookshelf. He had given Ross many of them as presents.

Ross perched on his bed like a gargoyle, silent, stiff and alert.

"So, what's going on, Ross Sauce? Your Mom's worried about you."

Ross barely lifted his shoulder in response.

Uncle Tim wheeled closer to the bed, orienting his chair toward the window and the closet like his nephew. "Dude, I can't help if you don't tell me what's going on."

Ross glanced at his uncle, then resumed his contemplation.

"Okay, your Mom said there's something bothering you in the closet. Show me."

Ross moved, arms tight to his body, head low, his eyes never leaving the corner of the room with its brown wood door and antique knob. Uncle Tim's chair whistled as he made his way there. He turned the handle and threw open the door with a thump against the wall.

Inside, well-organized objects and tidy clothes hung in the cedar-lined space. Ross backed behind his Uncle's chair and pointed over his shoulder with a shaking index finger. He whispered, "Do you see it? There, on the middle shelf?"

Uncle Tim shivered. "What is it, Ross?"

He drew closer to his uncle, finding comfort in the warmth emanating from his shoulder. He whispered, afraid to draw the thing's attention. "A rat. It is right there." The rat opened its blood-red mouth and showed sharp teeth.

Uncle Tim pulled Ross to his side. Ross dragged his feet. He wanted to be brave for his uncle, but his insides quaked. He felt the urge to pee.

"Ross, whatever it is, you have to face it, man, no matter how hard."

Tears raced down his face, and a solid ball formed high in his throat. The shaking grew to convulsions. Uncle Tim pulled the boy onto his lap, holding him close. Ross continued to stare, barely blinking, into the shadowy alcove.

"What the hell is it? Tell me, Ross. What is the rat?"

Ross looked his Uncle in the eye, his voice a skeletal whisper. The rat screamed, trying to prevent the words. Once the emotional flood-gates opened, they rushed with snot and tears, dripping feelings of guilt and disgust.

"He touches me. He said I could never tell, that he'd hear me. He pushes me into the closet. He said no one would believe me…"

Uncle Tim held his nephew, stiffening with each disclosure. His stony face revealed nothing, but his eyes raged. When Ross finished, Uncle Tim said, "Listen to me. I knew a rat like that. He did bad things to me in my closet, too."

Ross' eyes widened. He licked his lips, feeling parched. He whispered, "Who was it? Who was the rat, Uncle Tim?"

Uncle Tim blinked back tears. "Your grandfather."

Ross gasped. Chills prickled his arms, and he felt sick. Grandfather's leathery skin and dried lips had scratched. His watery eyes had stared, and his scaly tongue flicked, lecherous. His voice sounded tiny as a suppressed memory. "Pap?"

Uncle Tim nodded. "In life, sometimes bad things happen, and sometimes monsters do more than live in your closet." He kissed the top of Ross' head. "The damned rat is dead. It died of old age. It can't hurt anyone now. It can't hurt you anymore."

The rat blurred as Ross' tears poured unchecked over his chin and dripped to his t-shirt. When he finished, exhausted, trembling, nauseated, the rat vanished for good.

Index

Several of the short stories in this collection first appeared in other publications. My thanks to those who published my words!

The following stories were first published as noted.

All of the Haikus were written for #horrorhaikutuesday on Twitter hosted by Jeannette Andromeda

ABOUT THE AUTHOR

Kerry E.B. Black writes from an over-stuffed little house in the land where Romero's Dead roamed. She has long loved words and entices them to create tales both fanciful and true. Hailing from a small suburb situated along a fog-enshrouded river outside of a City of Steel and Bridges, Kerry incorporates Yankee sensibilities and a strong work ethic into every project.

Her children think she's dull, and their dogs agree, but the family cats, Poe and Hemingway, feel differently. The felines find a kinship with their nocturnal buddy and encourage Kerry to write.

Some of Kerry's works have crept into anthologies and literary journals. She writes for *Games Omniverse* and is a proud Rough Writer at *Carrot Ranch*. This one-time participant of the *One Year of Letters* project also served as a first reader for *Postcard Poems and Prose*. Kerry welcomes you to follow her other social media sites.

www.facebook.com/authorKerryE.B.Black
https://twitter.com/BlackKerryblick
https://www.goodreads.com/Kerry_E_B_Black